Vote for Garfy!

A Garfy Book

DAVID WILLERS AND CATE CARUTH

The Book Guild Ltd

First published in Great Britain in 2021 by
The Book Guild Ltd
9 Priory Business Park
Wistow Road, Kibworth
Leicestershire, LE8 0RX
Freephone: 0800 999 2982
www.bookguild.co.uk
Email: info@bookguild.co.uk
Twitter: @bookguild

Typeset in Minion Pro

Printed and bound in Great Britain by CPI Group (UK) Ltd, Croydon, CR0 4YY

ISBN 978 1913551 964

British Library Cataloguing in Publication Data.
A catalogue record for this book is available from the British Library.

To Sammy

Dedicated to the real Garfield,
still loved and missed every day.

Contents

1

Vote for Garfy!

Garfield Abercrombie Reginald Fergusson was an elegant ginger cat, with a white bib and socks and some very smart stripes down his back. Proud from the day he was born, Garfy would spend hours keeping his stripes in tip-top condition and neatly lined up.

If you hadn't met him before, you might think that Garfy was an ordinary, friendly, ginger tom. You might not realise that he was Ely's number one celebri-cat, famous throughout the city, from the threshold of Paterson's modern superstore to the ancient stone doorstep of the cathedral.

To David, the human whom Garfy allowed to live with him, the elegant ginger cat would always be a hero, even when his escapades caused chaos!

Garfy enjoyed riding in people's cars, catching trains to far-off places and being the talk of the city, but most of all, he loved the humans and all their strange ways.

There were cat-lovers galore in Ely and the most loved was Garfy. Wherever he went, there was always someone to pet him and always a little treat or two.

Nowhere else in the whole of the United Kingdom was a cat so famous and so adored. Nowhere else would children willingly go shopping with their parents. Most children hated walking around supermarkets, pushing trollies, loading them up with food and other things for the house for what seemed like hours, then taking all the groceries out again for them to be scanned, to then be put back again into bags, *then* to the car, *then* back home to the cupboards. It seemed such a lot of work for people to do, and they would do it every week, sometimes more! Going to Paterson's was different. Children would happily go, just to seek out Garfy and play hide and seek between the aisles.

***

Not everyone liked Garfy, though. Mr Bennet, Paterson's store manager, disliked him intensely. As far as he was concerned, Garfy had ruined most of last year for him. The curious cat had muscled in on the opening of the superstore, upsetting the very important person who was there to open it. He had made a mess of the aisles fighting with another cat, bitten a child at Christmas of all times and had embarrassed Mr Bennet in front of Emma, the regional manager.

Secretly, though, even Mr Bennet knew that Garfy was good for the store. Because of him, Paterson's was a roaring success and saw most customers out of all the Paterson's up and down the country. Mrs Paterson had given him a pay rise because of it, although she ignored his pleas for a bigger office. So, he did his best to ignore Garfy and keep out of his way. He simply pretended the ginger tom didn't exist and refused to speak about him to anyone else.

But there was someone who detested Garfy more than anyone else. Someone who resented the elegant ginger tom so much, he tried to have cats banned from Paterson's.

Garfy set off his allergies, making him sneeze, cough and wheeze. Garfy had upstaged him at one of the most important tasks he had undertaken and made him the laughing stock of Ely. He was a *Very Important Person* and, as far as he was concerned, Garfy had made him out to be unimportant. The *Very Important Person*, the person who had opened Paterson's (or tried to open it before Garfy turned up to steal the show), was none other than Josh Batt, the local councillor.

***

Spring had come again to the city. The blossom on the trees in Cherry Hill Park had grown so thick and lush that when a gust of wind caught the branches, it fell like pink confetti all over the passers-by. The Easter holidays were about to start and everyone was getting ready to celebrate with egg hunts, picnics and feasts.

It was also the time of the local elections, when people decided whom they wanted to be Ely's mayor.

Josh Batt, of course, was running in the elections and he desperately wanted to become mayor. He thought that would make him important again.

When you think about being mayor, it's a good idea to come up with a list of things you are going to do when you are elected. That is exactly what Josh Batt was doing, sitting in his study. He wasn't exactly thinking of all the good things he could bring to the residents of Ely, though; he was thinking about all the things that would make him seem important. He sat there with his fine bone china mug with the Batt coat of arms on it, staring at the big map of the city he had pasted up on the wall. What were the kind of things could he think up for his campaign? He looked more and more intently at the map as ideas formed in his head.

It was then he caught sight of Paterson's on the map and the memories of *that cat* came flooding back. Then he noticed a patch of ground to the side of Paterson's that didn't seem to be doing anything much but had lots of potential – lots of potential to make him very popular. Josh grinned as he started typing furiously on his computer. Soon, he had his ideas written down and, with a hard tap of the return key, he sent the document to the local paper. This would be his return to the spotlight, he thought. With all these ideas, he would win the campaign and become mayor of Ely.

***

A computer at the office of the *Ely Enquirer* came suddenly to life. *Bing!* There was a new email waiting to be read.

Ameena, the editor, peered at the screen as she read its contents. "Interesting," she said with a smile, "very interesting."

She set to work assigning the story to one of her writers. "For the front page," she wrote. "Can you complete it in two days, ready for Friday's edition?" She was sure the story was going to capture a lot of people's attention over the weekend.

***

The week went by without much incident. Garfy made his daily trips to Paterson's to sit in his favourite spot, a pile of towels, and receive guests. The children who came to the supermarket made a beeline for the homeware aisle, where they hoped their favourite cat would be.

Sure enough, he would be there, and sure enough, the children would make a fuss of him and sneak him treats. He was careful not to eat too many (it was important to stay fit and healthy) and would leave the unopened packets for Evan, the homewares assistant. Evan would take them to the front of the store to put in the donation box for the local cat shelter. Apart from his visits though, nothing much else occurred. Garfy reflected on his steady routine, feeling slightly bored by the calm and quiet and wondering what to do with himself to make life interesting.

He didn't have to wait too long to find out.

***

Friday morning came and, after a sumptuous breakfast of tuna and kibble, Garfy decided to curl up on David's lap and have forty winks before the day started. He had to fight for space with the newspaper, already open and laid across David's knees.

"Humph!" thought Garfy. "Why do I always have to fight for a space here?" In his frustration, he began trampling the edge of the newspaper in the hope that David would notice, give him some space on his lap and maybe rub his cheeks.

David was rather distracted this morning though, and kept trying to move Garfy off the paper.

He tutted. "You're not going to like this, Garfy. You're not going to like it at all."

Garfy looked at him. What was it that he wasn't going to like?

He stared at front page of the *Ely Enquirer*, following David's gaze, and he began to get very annoyed. His tail swished from left to right and he paced up and down, not quite knowing what to do with his frustration.

"This will not do! Not in my city," he thought at last. He jumped down from David's lap and darted out of the cat flap. This needed sorting, right now!

***

Mr Bennet had the same paper in front of him in his office at the back of Paterson's. As he read it, a grin spread slowly across his face.

Now, no one would ever describe him as a cheery man, so the smile on his face was most unusual. Nobody could see him or even hear him for that matter, so he let out a little chuckle.

"Well, this will disrupt everything," he said to himself. "What a marvellous start to the spring!"

***

Written across the front page of the *Ely Enquirer* was what Josh Batt had sent from his laptop only a few days ago, to Ameena at the newspaper. It was a list of promises he was making if he became mayor.

And *what* a list of promises! Some seemed too good to be true.

Among the many proposals, he wanted to encourage more people to come to Ely, so they could spend their time in the shops and make more money for local businesses.

More people visiting meant more cars, and more cars meant more car parks were needed, so Josh proposed four more car parks on the outskirts of the city, one very close to Paterson's. He wanted a bigger, faster road all around the city too, so that people could get to it more easily.

His list was all about making more money.

Last on the list, though, was what had made Mr Bennet smile and Garfy miss his morning nap.

Josh Batt was promising a lot more for dogs and their owners across the city. He was proposing that dog owners could take their pets everywhere in the city and 'dog zones' were to be created in every shop, where they could have a place to play and rest while their owners shopped.

***

Now Ely has a large proportion of cat-lovers but in equal measure, some believe, there are lovers of dog. Many a Saturday afternoon you would see dogs and humans on long walks together. They were allowed in some shops but it was well-known that people had asked for more to be done for dogs to be welcomed in all areas of the centre.

Of particular interest to Mr Bennet though, was the proposal that the main 'dog zone' be set up on the land which was right in front of Paterson's. Dogs could come and play with other dogs, have meals and generally be fussed over. There would be a special grooming parlour and a large park area for them to exercise.

"Ha!" said Mr Bennet in satisfaction. Even though he didn't much like dogs, the idea of a dog zone would put an end to Garfy's visits to Paterson's once and for all.

Imagine Garfy trying to run the gauntlet of a whole host of dogs, just to get into the shop. Imagine him being snapped at from left and right all over Ely. Imagine the chase all those dogs would give to see him off whenever he came near.[1]

***

All across the city the newspaper was being read. People agreed that the list of promises, although ambitious, mostly seemed good ideas but they were worried for Garfy and the other city cats. Would they be safe anywhere with so many dog zones? Surely they should have *some* areas to themselves?

***

Garfy knew he was being pushed out of Ely. It was bad enough that Paterson's was built on his favourite roaming ground. That he could just about accept. After all, he was always welcome there now. But dogs?

---

1   It just goes to show how little Mr Bennet knew about cats. Have you ever seen a cat/dog standoff? Cats know how to stick up for themselves!

"No, this will not do!" thought Garfy.

It was no good. Something had to be done, and quick.

***

Garfy strode up the hill to the council offices, ready to protest.

Looking for a way in, he almost tripped someone up. It was Aleah D Bell.

Aleah was Josh Batt's old campaign manager from the last elections but she found him too difficult to work with. She had ended up working all day, every day and all weekend too, so she had no chance to do any of the things *she* wanted to do, let alone have the kind of adventures she so admired Garfy for.

"Hello, Garfy. I'm sorry I nearly tripped over you," said Aleah. She moved to the side and crouched down to scratch behind Garfy's ear. Garfy purred and nuzzled up against her.

They remained outside the council offices for some time, Aleah fussing and Garfy purring, until Aleah looked at her watch.

"Goodness!" she said. "Is that the time? I must be going! It was so lovely to see you again, Garfy. Run along home now, it's nearly lunchtime."

Garfy didn't move an inch.

"What is it? I don't suppose you want to run for mayor, do you? Is that why you're here?" she said, half joking.

Garfy kept looking at the front door of the council offices.

"Garfy? Do you really?" Aleah bent down again. "Well, my goodness. If that's the case, you've just got yourself a campaign manager. I'll help you win that election!"

***

Night and day, Aleah and Garfy worked on the campaign (but not weekends!). They planned out every idea that Garfy had as they looked at how they could make Ely a better place.

At last they had written down everything in an email and sent it straight to the offices of the *Ely Enquirer*.

Bing! It reached Ameena as quick as a flash.

"Even more interesting," she said.

***

The next Friday, emblazoned across the front of the *Ely Enquirer* was Garfy's face and the news that he was running for mayor.

What a stir it caused all weekend!

It was a bold move for anyone to want to be mayor and go up against Josh Batt but for a cat to seek election? This was news indeed!

Although Garfy's campaign was less ambitious than Josh Batt's, it was just as attractive. He wanted more to be done about the environment, so he proposed litter-picking days for everyone, more buses for people to get around, equality for all pets, a new park with swings and a boating lake, new homes for older people with gardens

11

and a picnic area for their families when they came to visit.

***

Josh Batt was drinking his morning coffee as he read the *Ely Enquirer* that morning. When he saw the headline, he was so shocked he sprayed coffee all over his desk.

What was that cat doing now? The very idea of Garfy set off his allergies and he was determined not to let the ginger tom become mayor.

But how to stop him?

As Josh looked down at the official reports and papers he had to deal with that day, he saw the list of rules for the upcoming election. A little grin flashed across his face.

"Yes, of course. He won't have enough money!"

***

Now, wanting to run in an election means a lot of things. You have to have a list of improvements you want to make, you need a team who will help you and you must be prepared to work closely with the council all year to help make people's lives better.

All of this Garfy knew and was willing to do.

What he'd forgotten, however, was that when you put your name forward to become mayor, you have to give some money to the council. It's called a deposit.

Garfy didn't have that amount of money. Garfy didn't have *any* money. He was a cat! He didn't want to ask David because Garfy knew he saving up for their next trip to the seaside.

What was Ely's most famous cat going to do?

***

What Garfy didn't know was that Aleah was already on the case. She talked to everyone they knew about raising the money. Some people donated the change in their pockets; others were able to give a little more from purses and wallets. The children who regularly visited Garfy at Paterson's even raided their piggy banks and gave it all to him.

But it still wasn't enough.

It looked like Garfy would have to give up and let Josh Batt win.

On the last day before candidates had to pay their deposits so they could stand in the election, a call came in to Aleah's mobile. She listened intently to the person on the other end of the phone.

"Yes… yes. I see. Right… OK, thank you very much." She pressed a button to end the call and looked at Garfy intently.

That was it, Garfy knew it. He couldn't go on. Someone had called and told them to stop campaigning; they didn't have enough money.

"That was Mrs Fredericks," said Aleah. Mrs Fredericks was last year's mayor and she had never seen eye-to-eye with Josh Batt. "She wants to help. She loves your campaign promises and she is going to make up the missing amount so you can run for mayor."

What good news to end the week on. The word travelled fast around Ely and reached Josh just as he left his offices.

"Bother that cat!" he said. He would have to think up something else to stop Garfy taking over and becoming mayor.

***

Monday came and Garfy's campaign was in full swing. He arranged to meet Aleah at nine o'clock sharp to prepare for the week ahead. If he was going to be mayor and keep the needs of cats in Ely on an equal footing with dogs, he needed to talk to as many people as possible to get their support.

He hastily finished his breakfast, skipping his morning nap on David's lap. He had to stop Josh Batt putting car parks over all the lovely green areas in the city. Most importantly, he had to stop dogs taking over!

Aleah had everything prepared. They were going to spend the whole day telling people about his ideas and listen to people talk about theirs. The one thing she had learned from the way Josh Batt did things was to listen to others and pay attention to what they thought.

***

They started outside Paterson's – far enough away so as not to annoy people but near enough so they could talk to shoppers going in and out.

An older couple, Mr and Mrs Deaver, thought that Garfy's idea about some small houses with neat little gardens being built near the shops and doctor's surgery sounded good, but they did think that Josh Batt's plans for dog zones was splendid, especially the one planned for outside the supermarket.

They had a Pekinese dog called Ralph and they really didn't like leaving him at home when they went shopping because he got lonely. They couldn't leave him in the car because, unlike Garfy, Ralph hated cars.

Garfy thought that Ralph sounded a bit soft – what was not to like about cars? Think of all the fun you could have riding around in the comfy seats, looking out of the window with one paw up as if you were royalty, waving to everyone going by.

He didn't say this to Mr and Mrs Deaver, though.

The twins, Charlotte and Sasha Beresford, made a huge fuss of Garfy when they came to the front of the store, so much so that he got distracted and missed some of what their parents were saying. Thank goodness Aleah was taking notes.

Later she told him that the Beresfords were delighted with Garfy's ideas. They didn't like the idea of car parks taking up all of Ely and they believed that pet equality was much fairer than just giving dogs priority.

Garfy was doing the right thing, they felt.

Aleah and Garfy moved to the town centre after lunch, to talk to the people in and around the shops there.

Some loved the idea of Garfy being the mayor.

"That would stop the likes of Josh Batt laying tarmac over Ely," said Celeste, the manager of the dance studio, "and you'd always be welcome in here, Garfy!"

But others…?

Colonel Oakeshott thought it was the silliest thing he'd ever heard. "A cat as mayor? Not in my day; no, sir!"

Garfy was doing his best but by the end of the day, he was exhausted. He felt dizzy from looking up at all the humans. He must have listened to hundreds!

**

The following day brought bad news. Josh Batt had indeed thought of something else to stop Garfy's campaign.

He had spent the weekend looking up the newspaper articles about Garfy over the last year, trying to dig up anything he could use against him and he had found something he just knew would stop 'that cat' in his tracks.

The previous autumn Garfy had shot to fame and become very conceited about it. His reputation had reached far and wide and he had thought this made him very important indeed.

Garfy felt ashamed just thinking about all the people he had upset.

Josh Batt was in the town campaigning and reminding everyone how badly behaved Garfy had been. "Do we really want someone like that being mayor, sitting on a silk cushion and being all aloof?"

Some people shook their heads, remembering how snooty Garfy had been after being interviewed for the television. No, it wouldn't do at all to have someone like that representing Ely.

Maybe Josh Batt *was* the best thing for the city after all.

***

Garfy was devastated and slunk off down the hill, back past Paterson's and his huge portrait in the foyer, and back to David's lap. He felt sure he had lost already.

As the cat flap settled behind him, he saw that someone was sitting with David, waiting for him to come home.

It was Aleah!

"I remember what happened too, Garfy," she said. "But I also remember how your portrait was auctioned and you made £10,000 to save the local cat shelter."

Garfy beamed at Aleah. She really was good at this – better than he was.

This was Aleah's plan: Garfy would release a statement just ahead of election day to remind people how sorry he was for the upset he had caused last year and how he had made up for it by raising money for charity. Any money he made out of being mayor would also go straight to the shelter. There would be no posh silken cushions and no strutting around pretending he owned the place!

***

Lots of residents still believed in Garfy.

Jon, the owner of the flower shop, had rosettes made out of the off-cuts of beautiful ribbons he used to make bouquets. He had them neatly arranged all across the front of his window.

Zachariah's, the toy shop, had taken their Easter display down to fill the window with orange and white

balloons, the same colour as Garfy's ginger stripes, with an enormous sign that said, "VOTE FOR GARFY!"

The photo shop had printed out a copy of the portrait that hung in Paterson's and pasted it inside their window.

Garfy felt encouraged by this, but Colonel Oakeshott and his friends were still not convinced. "I'm sorry, Garfy, but a cat as mayor? It's just not going to work."

To be honest, a tiny part of Garfy agreed. There was so much to do and so many things that people seemed to want and need from their mayor. How could one cat do all that?

Garfy was determined that Josh Batt and his dog idea wouldn't take over, however, especially now, when he had been so mean to Garfy.

Besides, if Garfy didn't run against him, who would?

***

On the last day of campaigning, Garfy worked hard in and around the city, proudly wearing his rosette. He kissed babies, played with string that children dangled in front of him and helped to pick litter in the park with all his friends and neighbours. It was exhausting work but it was worth it.

As Aleah walked him home, she said, "I've really enjoyed working with you, Garfy, thank you." She bent down and kissed him on the top of his head.

Garfy sighed as he went through the cat flap. It had been really been great working with Aleah but he was so tired from it all, he didn't know if he could keep it up for a whole year. Aleah seemed to have so much more energy than he did.

David prepared him a special supper of mackerel and they snoozed on the sofa together for the rest of the evening.

***

Election day was a sunny May morning. Garfy had been awake for what seemed like hours and he was getting more nervous by the minute.

He pinned on his rosette to give him courage and walked slowly to the council offices, where the candidates were being interviewed by the press and where the results would be announced later.

All across Ely people were queuing at the polling booths. Some had got up extra early so they could vote before they went to work. Others had prepared snacks and picnics to eat in the line if it turned out to be a long wait. Still others were planning to vote after work, stopping off on their way home.

All day long, people lined up, chatting in the queues, wondering who would win.

It was the highest ever turn-out for an election. Charlotte and Sasha even set up their own unofficial voting booths for children and animals to vote, they were so excited by it all.

Garfy had had that effect, if nothing else: he showed how important it was to be part of a community.

The day was slow and long, as were the queues outside the polling stations. Garfy tried very hard to be chirpy and positive all day but there were a couple of times he had to slink off and have forty winks underneath a tree or a nearby pram in the queue. All that campaigning was very hard going for a cat.

***

Evening finally arrived and the polling stations closed. The boxes all came back to the council offices and the count began.

For what seemed like hours, the officials counted every paper. Then they would gather up the piles and pass them to another team who would count them all over again. It seemed an endless process but, finally, every paper had been counted and tied up in bundles and the numbers were ready to announce.

A microphone was set up outside the council offices for the announcement. The car park at the front was so crowded with people that they were spilling out onto the road and the police had to come and direct traffic to keep everyone safe.

It seemed like all of Ely had come to find out who had won. Dog owners brought their beagles and schnauzers and terriers with them. Cat owners brought their Siamese and bobtails and Maine Coons with them.

It was a very tight squeeze.

***

An official stepped up to the microphone. Garfy could hardly breathe. Aleah stroked his fur gently to keep him calm.

"Welcome, everyone, to the election of the new mayor of Ely."

Everyone was looking from Josh Batt to Garfy.

Josh Batt smiled out at them, sure he had won already. Garfy tried not to meet anyone's eye.

The announcer continued. "I hereby declare that the number of votes for each candidate for the position for mayor of Ely is as follows…" Everyone held their breath.

"Joshua Caleb Batt, 5,820."

It was going to be close!

"Garfield Abercrombie Reginald Fergusson, 6,467."

"What?" thought Garfy. "What? I won? Did I win?" A loud uproarious cheer came from the crowd.

"Three cheers for Garfy!" someone shouted.

Josh Batt was red with rage. So much so that he stomped off into the council offices to sulk.

Garfy was picked up and raised high above the heads of everyone there. "Hip hip, hooray!"

Garfy had won! He was now His Right Worshipful, the Mayor of Ely. My goodness he had a lot of work to do!

***

The celebrations didn't last long, however. Josh Batt came striding back out of the council offices with a very big grin and very dusty old book in his arms.

He grabbed the microphone. "Not so fast! Why no one thought to check this before is beyond me." His fingers traced the words on the page as he read: "The statutes of Ely clearly state that only *humans* can be elected mayor. The election is void!"

Everyone groaned. Garfy had only been mayor for five minutes and now he'd had his title taken away – just like that.

"Unfair!" shouted someone in the crowd.

The announcing councillor took his glasses out of his top pocket and peered at the book. There was complete silence while he examined the statutes of Ely with care.

"I'm afraid Mr Batt is correct. I hearby announce the election null and void. There will be another election in due course." With that, he turned and scurried off back to the council offices.

***

Don't tell anyone, but Garfy actually didn't mind not being mayor. He didn't think he was cut out for politics after all.

He was so tired from all the campaigning, all the talking and listening and work, that all he wanted to do was curl up on his favourite lap, without the bother of a newspaper to compete with! He wanted the simple life again: a tuna breakfast, his favourite spot in Paterson's and a friendly neighbourhood.

***

In fact, the new elections for mayor were organised very quickly, campaigning was over and done with and voting was logged.

And the winner?

No, not Josh Batt, though he did come a respectable second.

The new mayor, the Worshipful Mayor of Ely, was none other than Aleah D Bell! She had so loved Garfy's plans that she decided to stand on the same platform to put them in place. Once she was elected her first job was not for cats *or* for dogs. It wasn't for *any* pets, in fact, but to build the lovely houses for older people, with beautiful gardens, a pond and picnic area.

Garfy thoroughly approved and often visited the gardens. In fact, plenty of cat *and* dog lovers would use the gardens, where there was plenty of space for animals of all kinds.

It just goes to show, whatever the politicians say and do, people will find a way to live and enjoy life together.

2

Gardening Garfy

As the summer approached and the weather got warmer, everyone in Ely began to come outside to enjoy the sun.

Garfy had never understood why humans did not seem to go outside in the winter. Of course, he liked to be warm and cosy but he also wanted to get outside and go for a run every day. That was why he made his daily visits to Paterson's, whatever the weather. It had to be said though, when it was cold he did take the most direct route and didn't linger on the way. Now though, the sun rose early and set late so the elegant ginger tom took longer and more interesting routes to the supermarket for his mid-morning inspection.

One of his most frequent and favourite routes was through Churchill Gardens, a small street filled with twenty or so little houses. He liked it so much, he went that way several times a week.

He weaved his way through the houses for two reasons. First, it was such a pretty place to walk and second, the people who lived in the houses were so nice. They always had a kind word, a wave or a little treat for Garfy.

The path through the houses was lined with a small verge and, in amongst the neatly trimmed grass, someone had planted all kinds of flowers. In the spring there were nodding yellow daffodils and in the summer emerged a lush carpet of daisies. Then came a bold flush of dahlias, each flower a bright yellow in the middle turning to a bold orange at the tip of every petal. At their most open they looked like they were on fire. Even in the winter there were snowdrops bravely standing up to the cold.

The beautifully kept front gardens were just as appealing. Every one of them was fit to bursting. There were flowers, bushes and plants of all kinds; so many that Garfy had a feeling the gardens were all in friendly competition with each other for which was the fullest and most beautiful!

***

The residents of Churchill Gardens were always busy in their gardens – planting seeds, trimming, pruning, digging and weeding – all to make them neat and pretty.

Benjamin and Edna had set a two-seater bench against the wall of their house, so that they could sit and look at their garden together. Just as the sun set every day, the light would shine on their faces, warming their skin and making them happy and sleepy. Their home was welcoming and always ready to receive members of their large family, so the bench often held a grandchild or two in the early afternoon.

There they would sit, on Edna's lap, listening to stories from far-off lands with desert sunsets and huge billowing tents. Leaning into the garden from the borders, as if they too were listening to the stories, were tall shrubs that welcomed all manner of butterflies and bees, flitting and buzzing through the flowers. Garfy loved to push himself into the garden through the shrubs and flowers. There he amused himself by playing with the children and sneaking up on the insects whenever they landed.

Kofi and Georgia's gravel path up to their front door was made of sparkling black stones and, in amongst the tall purple irises overlooking the path, were two statues. One stood tall, holding a staff in his right hand. He had a man's body and the head of a falcon. The second sat on the other side of the path. It was a large black cat and at his feet Georgia had planted sweet-smelling herbs where Garfy liked to sit, sleeping in the sun.

Ali and Caroline welcomed Garfy into their garden whenever they saw him. They had built a small platform on which they had put a small bed for their ancient cat, Thomas. Thomas padded outside whenever it was warm enough and would lie in the sun all day.

Garfy liked to visit the elderly cat before he went to Paterson's to find out if he could fetch his friend anything from there. Thomas was usually quite content and seldom asked for anything but he enjoyed Garfy's brief company. They didn't speak much; just sitting together was enough for the old cat.

Ali had begun to design something out of the box hedge she and Caroline had planted some years ago. It was beginning to take shape but Garfy couldn't work out what it was. It seemed to be a collection of blobs and lumps and strange wiggly bits.

Garfy adored every bit of walking through Churchill Gardens. Such lovely gardens and such nice people.

***

The nicest people with the loveliest garden lived two doors away from the main road that Garfy crossed each time he went to Paterson's. Kenji and Hana lived there and had done ever since Garfy could remember.

They were the kindest and happiest people anyone had the pleasure to meet. And what a garden they had! Most people who know about these things would call it a *typical English cottage garden*. To Garfy it was his idea of heaven.

It was a much larger plot than the other gardens and they had filled it to the very edges. There was a small pond to the right of the path, with tall proud lilies around the edge. In the pond were tiny orange fish that Garfy liked to watched darting in and out of the sunbeams. Next to the pond, a small tree had been planted when they moved there and now it towered over the garden and gave shade to the pond dwellers and lily-of-the-valley plants.

On the far side of the garden, up against the fence, grew a rambling rose heavy with bright red flowers. It was so big now that every summer it tried to grow right into the open window of the kitchen. Planted beside it were hollyhocks, foxgloves and delphiniums, and below, aquilegias of many different colours.

It wasn't only Garfy who enjoyed walking through the houses. People would walk that way too, usually slowing down to look at all the beautiful flowers and bushes and trees. As they reached Kenji and Hana's garden many would stop.

"Stunning," some would say, and, "So pretty!" and, "How lovely."

Children walking to the nearby school would often stop and stare, fascinated by the butterflies dancing around the flowers, until their parents hurried them along before the school bell went. The gardens were so beautiful, they were responsible for making quite a few people late as they paused to admire the gorgeous display.

***

Kenji and Hana were always out in their garden, snipping and tidying and sweeping the path. When people stopped, they would bow low to them in greeting. They loved their English cottage garden, for they had quite a different one where they used to live.

You see, Kenji and Hana moved to Ely from Japan, from a city called Takayama. They had a small house there too and the garden had a cool pond and tall trees, mossy rocks, a little bridge and raked sand in swirling rows and circles. It was a very calming place and was admired by all their neighbours.

When they moved to Ely they wanted to try something different and soon found that they enjoyed gardening this way just as much as they did in their Japanese garden.

***

As summer progressed, Garfy walked passed Kenji and Hana's garden most mornings and noticed that, at the beginning of the season it had been lush and colourful, with everything blooming beautifully. Now though, the rambling rose looked like it had had a growth spurt and was knocking on the kitchen window, wanting to come in. It had grown all the way along the windowsill and towards the door. The blossoms were looking tired too and the pond had lots of petals floating on the surface. The garden was starting to look a bit untidy.

Garfy thought nothing of it, however, and went on to Paterson's.

By the next week, things began to look a lot worse. Garfy met Ali standing in front of the rose, cutting it back and tutting quietly.

"Poor Kenji," she whispered.

"Poor Kenji?" thought Garfy. Whatever was the matter?

Ali saw him staring into the garden. "Oh, Garfy. Kenji is poorly. He'll be up and about soon though, I'm sure," but she didn't look very sure. In fact, she looked worried.

The neighbours did their best to help but, between looking after their own gardens, looking after grandchildren, working and going on their summer holidays, they couldn't keep up with Kenji and Hana's garden. It had started to look overgrown and ragged.

***

Garfy himself went on holiday in the middle of summer when he and David took their annual trip to the seaside. The week seemed to go too quickly, as most holidays do, but he was excited to come home to see all his friends again.

The morning after they arrived back, Garfy trotted down the road to visit with the residents of Churchill Gardens. It looked like everyone had been busy while he was away.

Benjamin and Edna had painted their two-seater bench a light blue colour to match the cornflowers popping up everywhere. "Hello, Garfy!" they called. "Lovely to see you back."

"Did you have a nice holiday?" Kofi and Georgia asked him as he went by. They were picking herbs from around the statues to add to a big pot that was simmering away in their kitchen, ready for their visiting family.

Ali and Caroline had at last finished the sculptures they were making out of the box hedge in their garden. On one side was the shape of Thomas, lying down, his paw across his face. On the other side sitting up, looking proudly out onto the path was the outline of an elegant cat with smart stripes down his back. Garfy was so surprised! They had the exact likeness of him. He miaowed loudly in delight. What a wonderful present to come back to. How he enjoyed coming here to see all his friends.

Of course, he had saved his favourite garden until last – the house two doors away from the main road. Off he trotted to see Kenji and Hana.

***

As soon as he reached the edge of the house he saw that something was wrong. The rambling rose had taken over and the pond was filled with rotting petals. The fish huddled together in one corner and most of the hollyhocks had blown over and died. The path was dirty and slimy with leaves.

What a mess! What was once the most stunning part of Churchill Gardens looked abandoned.

"We tried," said Ali, as she caught up with Garfy. Just as she spoke, the front door opened and they could see a face peering round it.

It was Hana. How nice it was to see her again, thought Garfy. He perked up a bit at the sight of her and wondered where Kenji was. He didn't have to wonder for long.

Hana opened the door wider and stood aside. Behind her was a metal frame, moving very, very slowly. Behind the metal frame was a man, bent over and shuffling.

"Who is that?" thought Garfy. "And where is Kenji?"

He didn't realise that the slow-moving man, now lifting his leg over the threshold with a lot of effort, was his old friend.

Garfy couldn't believe what he saw. No longer was Kenji soft-faced and smiling. He frowned in concentration, trying hard not to slip or trip as he stepped into the garden.

Garfy's heart sank as he realised why the much-loved garden now looked so unloved.

Kenji was very poorly and had been in hospital all these weeks. Hana had been going to see him every day but it took her a long time to get there on the bus and a long journey home. So much so that she didn't have the time or the energy to keep the garden looking lovely.

The neighbours tried to help but they couldn't manage to do all of it.

"Hana told me that the garden is too much for them now and they need a garden with a lot less maintenance. Whatever can we do?" Ali whispered.

Garfy didn't know. What he did know was that he would find a way to help them, no matter what.

***

Walking to Paterson's that day was slow-going. Garfy was sad to see Kenji's garden looking so overgrown but he was even sadder to see that Kenji himself was so ill. How could he and his neighbours possibly help him and his garden?

When he reached the foyer of Paterson's, he didn't go straight to his bale of towels, nor did he seek out any of his favourite shop assistants for a cuddle. He didn't even feel particularly like playing with the children who came to find him. He just walked aimlessly round not knowing what to do.

He was so preoccupied that he hadn't even noticed the new display at the front of the superstore. When he bumped into it, it gave him quite a fright. It was a life-sized cardboard cut-out of a man standing with one hand on his hip, a large hardback book in his other hand. Garfy didn't know who he was but he looked quite friendly. He was wearing great big green wellies and was standing on what looked like a mound of freshly dug earth.

Garfy jumped again when someone announced over a loudspeaker, "Timmy Welch is touring all of Paterson's superstores signing his new book. His last visit will be Ely, where he will be announcing the winner of his garden makeover competition. Don't miss your chance to enter the competition. Just fill in your details at the front of the shop, where you can also pick up his new book *Gardening for Everyone.*"

"Ah!" thought Garfy. "So this is Timmy Welch." He'd seen him when David was watching television, turning rundown land into lovely gardens. An idea began to form in his brain. His paws began to tingle and his tail stood to attention.

That was how he was going to help Kofi and Hana. They could enter the competition to have their garden made pretty again. But Hana wouldn't leave Kofi to come down to Paterson's to fill in the form to enter.

This was going to be difficult. Garfy couldn't write that well because it was difficult to hold a pen in his paws, no matter how hard he tried.

***

Have you ever noticed that when you think that things are impossible, when you think a problem can't be solved, someone always appears to help?

Well, this happened to Garfy quite often. Remember the time he got all the way to the seaside and didn't know how he was going to get home? Or the time when the big black cat Tyson threw him out of Paterson's and Garfy didn't know how he could make things better?

His friends were always there to help and this time was no exception. Just as Garfy was about to leave Paterson's for the day, downhearted that he couldn't think of an answer, Ali and Caroline came through the doors. They walked straight up to Timmy Welch's book display.

When they saw Garfy they waved. "Oh, what a good idea Garfy," said Caroline. "Let's put Kofi and Hana's name down. You never know, they might win!"

Garfy crossed his paws for good luck as Ali posted the form in the box. Just in time too, for Timmy Welch was coming to the store the very next day!

***

Garfy almost couldn't sleep for excitement! I say *almost* because Garfy could always sleep, no matter when or where it was! But he did have some very strange dreams that night, which kept waking him up.

He dreamed that he was wearing wellies, just like Timmy Welch's, one for each of his legs, each boot a different colour. In the dream he spent his time trotting around Kenji and Hana's garden, moving enormous boulders and dodging flying fish! He was glad to wake up safe and warm in his bed at home. He was also glad that he didn't have to wait too long to find out if they had won the garden makeover competition.

***

There was quite a crowd gathered at Paterson's. They were all there to see Timmy Welch, get their books signed and hear who had won the competition. Timmy was reading from his book already, so Garfy moved amongst the crowd to get a better look at this person.

He was a tall man with rosy cheeks and a friendly smile. He wore a brown chunky-knit jumper, faded blue jeans and, of course, his green wellies. Garfy did wonder why he was wearing wellies in a supermarket since Mr

Bennet made absolutely sure that the floor was sparkling clean every morning. The floor wasn't the least bit wet and the store manager certainly wouldn't allow any form of mud to come in. Nevertheless, Garfy thought Mr Welch seemed a nice person and, from the amount of books he was signing, he looked like he knew a lot about gardening.

Garfy crossed his paws again.

Just at that moment, Timmy caught sight of him. "Well," he said, "what have we here? What a lovely fellow!"

Timmy told the crowd how much he loved cats and how he had three of his own, all tortoiseshells. He made a fuss of Garfy as the ginger tom weaved in and out of his legs.

"But now," Timmy announced, stepping carefully around Garfy, "it is time to announce the winner of the garden makeover competition." He stood up as he was handed the box full of the entry slips.

A hush fell over the crowd. It seemed like everyone was holding their breath. Someone picked up Garfy so he could see.

Timmy reached his hand inside the box and brought a sole piece of paper out.

"Please let it be Kofi and Hana. *Please!*" thought Garfy.

"And the winner of the competition for a full garden makeover is... Amelie McCreedy from Cumbria! Congratulations, Amelie, I'll see you next month!"

***

There was such a lot of hustle and bustle after the announcement that Garfy became dizzy in the crowd of legs shuffling to and fro. He felt lost and overwhelmed. Kenji and Hana hadn't won, they wouldn't get a new garden and now they couldn't sit outside and enjoy their old garden because it was so overgrown. He didn't know what else to do except just sit there, in the middle of the milling crowds.

***

After all the books were signed and sold, everyone went about their business very quickly and the front of the shop was again empty. Garfy stood up and walked slowly to the door, his head down.

He hadn't felt this sad in such a long time. He really wanted to help Kenji and Hana, but it seemed that his chance had gone for good.

Timmy saw that the cat he had so admired earlier was still hanging around.

He approached Garfy. "Hello, young fella, are you still here? Lost?"

Garfy did indeed feel very lost.

"What a sad little cat you look." Timmy tickled him under his chin.

Usually the elegant cat loved a fuss but Garfy felt too unhappy to enjoy it today. He began to walk out again, his head down.

"Hey there, you do look sad. Have you really got lost? Can I help?"

Garfy didn't think so but Timmy seemed insistent. He followed Garfy out of the door but Garfy just wanted to go home.

***

When they reached the road, Garfy had an idea. Instead of going straight home, he could lead Timmy Welch to Churchill Gardens – then the gardener could see for himself.

"Paws crossed!" Garfy thought but without much hope.

Timmy did see, too. Garfy had managed to lead him all the way to Churchill Gardens and to the front of Kofi and Hana's garden.

"Oh dear!" said Timmy. "Is this where you live? No wonder you look so sad. What a mess."

The other residents noticed someone standing outside with Garfy and came out to see what was going on. When they saw who it was, they became very excited. Had Kenji and Hana won the makeover competition? Garfy looked so downcast, however, that they felt a little confused. Surely this was good news.

Someone brought a cup of tea out to Timmy and explained about Kenji being poorly, and how he had gone to hospital for an operation that morning. He wouldn't be back for another week. Caroline explained how much Kenji loved his garden but, with his illness, he and Hana weren't able to manage it any more.

The neighbours looked hopeful. Was Timmy here for the makeover?

"No, I'm afraid someone from Cumbria won the prize," said Timmy. "But I wonder..." He smiled. "I sold the most books out of all my tour visits today. You are all so nice and I have always loved Ely.

"I don't have to be in Cumbria for another two weeks. I rather fancy staying for a bit. What do you think, Garfy?"

Garfy looked up at him in surprise. Could Timmy be suggesting...?

"Yes, let's do it! If we all work together, it won't take long!"

The next two days went by in a whirr of planning and drawing and measuring and drinking tea.[2] At last they were ready.

On the third day, Garfy was woken up by a loud, "*Beep*, this vehicle in reversing! *Beep*, this vehicle is reversing!" It had begun.

Off he dashed, after the quickest breakfast he'd ever eaten, down to Churchill Gardens. There were Timmy and his crew bent over a large white sheet of paper. On the paper was a plan of how the team were going to transform Kenji and Hana's garden while they were away.

The beeping vehicle had been a lorry bulging with all manner of things for the project. It looked like there was so much in there, it would never fit in the garden without everything being piled on top of everything else.

All the neighbours were there to help. Benjamin and Edna had brought their children, their grandchildren and

---

2 Tea is very necessary for gardening, as anyone who knows about horticulture will tell you!

their grandchildren's friends to help out. Kofi and Georgia were on standby with tea and coffee, cake and sandwiches. Ali and Caroline had gathered everyone's tools, neatly marked so they could be returned to their owners at the end of the day.

Garfy was in awe. He didn't know how they could possibly change the rundown-looking garden into something that Kofi and Hana would be able to manage and enjoy.

Timmy and his crew unloaded the truck and out came a chainsaw, a spirit level, rakes and shovels. Each person there had at least one tool in their hand, ready to get to work. The design looked simple but there was so much to move out of the way first.

Nobody was happy about ripping up the plants that had been so lovingly grown from seed and cultivated but they knew that it would be worth it in the end. So, they started in the far corner, taking up dead plants and sifting out all the rubbish that had landed in the pond.

Garfy helped by scooping out the larger leaves from the pond until he could see the fish once more. They raced into the shadows as they saw the cat looming over them.

He looked at the plans regularly and Timmy consulted with him.

"What do you think, Garfy? Shall we put that boulder there? What about the awning? Just there? Or here?"

Garfy pawed the paper.

"Yes, that's what I think. Right, let's move that just a little to the right, please."

As the workers moved round the garden and cleared the ground, more and more plants piled up in the rubbish bins on the path. All except one.

***

Now that the garden was clear, wood was unloaded from the lorry. The long poles were concreted into the ground and a roof was fixed on top. This was going to be an open-fronted tea house, so that Kenji and Hana could be outside but sheltered from the rain and shaded from the sun. Next came paving slabs, laid all the way up to the front door. Around the path came shovels carrying golden gravel. Timmy built a bridge over the pond out of the leftover wood and the children painted it a bright shiny red. A small maple tree was planted next to the tree that had been grown from a sapling all those years ago.

Garfy supervised the planting of the rest of the garden. A cherry tree went in right at the end of the path and all along the side of the path they put forest grass. Rhododendrons and peonies and ferns were heeled in around the borders and in between, underneath the trees and up to the new fence, were piled cobblestones and gravel. To finish it all, the crew rolled down their long sleeves, put on thick gloves and teased the much-loved red rose up and over the tea house.

What a sight! On the one hand, a beautiful, neat and easy-to-look-after garden; on the other, mucky, very tired but very happy neighbours. Even Garfy's white bib and socks had turned a very unbecoming shade of brown!

Ali was the first to say it: "Garfy, you've done it again. What an amazing chap you are to help out your friends!"

***

Kenji had recovered so quickly in hospital that he was to come out the very next day. It wasn't long before they arrived back to Churchill Gardens but he and Hana were very apprehensive. What were they to do with their garden? It certainly wasn't going to be easy.

"If only we had a garden like the one in Takayama," said Hana. "We could maintain it easily."

Kenji had to agree but they were never going to do all that work without a miracle.

***

Well, a miracle it was! They walked slowly across the street from their car and, as they turned the corner, they couldn't believe all the people standing out on the path.

Had something happened? Had someone been burgled?

They were escorted to their door by Garfy, who had come to greet them.

What met them was a newly built and planted Japanese garden, just like the one they had back in Takayama. Kenji and Hana were delighted. Chairs were set up in the tea house and they sat down and admired everyone's hard work.

"We can't thank you enough," Kenji said, "but there is one way we can show our appreciation." Hana disappeared into the house. She came back out with a tray loaded with an iron teapot and lots of little teacups. She handed everyone a cup and went around filling them with steaming hot tea from the pot. They raised their cups and bowed low.

"*Arigato*." (Which, of course, is "thank you" in Japanese.)

What a wonderful way to end the day and start to Kenji's recovery, in their Japanese tea house, with their English rose growing overhead.

3

The Box Tizzy

Garfield Abercrombie Reginald Fergusson was an intelligent sort of cat. He was refined and smart and kept himself in good condition. He was (nearly) always well-behaved and had impeccable manners. He saw himself as well-to-do – a noble sort of fellow – but he wouldn't go as far as believing himself to be aristocratic.

David told him he was well-born – his mother and father were pure breeds, both ginger and white. His mother was an intelligent, sensible cat who kept a well-ordered, quiet life. His father had been more rebellious, however, and was always out for adventure (sound familiar?). He did tend toward laziness, which ended up being a constant source of argument between the two cats.

Apart from that, they lived their lives together and raised four litters of six cats each. Garfy was the only one left in Ely as his brothers and sisters were scattered around the country.

***

Although Garfy had much of his mother's temperament, in that he enjoyed a well-ordered life of tuna and kibble, visits to Paterson's superstore and long snoozes, he was just as happy with a bit of excitement in the company of friends, old and new. However, he did think that, although he wasn't always looking, adventure very often sought him out. Sometimes it seemed to happen quite by accident.

***

It was late summer now and the gardens all around Ely had started their last bloom. The sun was still warm and the wind still light but the days were getting shorter and everywhere the shops were reminding everyone, 'Back to School' and offering bargains on pens and paper.

Garfy loved these days more than anything. He liked to wander around lazily, looking for sunny spots to have forty winks.

On the Friday before the end of the summer holidays, Garfy did just that. He left David doing the crossword and headed out into the sun. He was in no hurry to be anywhere special, so he wandered down the road with no plans. It was quiet outside and Garfy met only a few people who stopped to say hello, tickle him behind his ears or scratch his head.

"Ah! This is nice!" he thought, as he trotted down towards Paterson's. On the route he had taken today, there was row of new houses with small front gardens. Some of them were laid to grass but one had been newly planted with flower beds and the smell coming from all the new plants was wonderful. Garfy couldn't get enough.

***

Have you ever heard about a plant called *napeta cataria*? Cats *love* it. It is their favourite plant. In fact, the common name is 'catnip'. They love it so much that they roll around on the ground rubbing themselves on the leaves.

Can you imagine a human doing that? What a sight that would be! People rolling around on the floor because they loved the smell of a plant so much.

Well, that's what catnip does for cats and that was the smell coming from the newly planted garden.

Garfy walked over.

It's smelled so good to him that he couldn't help but take a long breath in, with his face in the leaves. It was delicious and sweet and tangy all at the same time.

He rolled onto his back and played with the leaves.

He sprang back up and batted the stems so that the smell became even stronger all around him.

He buried his face in the whole plant, closing his eyes and rubbing his cheeks up against it.

He was in heaven.

He felt he didn't want to be anywhere else that day, he was so excited about his new discovery.

All morning Garfy played and batted and scratched at the catnip. He was having so much fun that he almost forgot about lunch but he didn't want to leave the catnip.

"Could I eat some of it for lunch?" he wondered.

Very carefully, he reached up and held a leaf between his teeth. Could he bite it? It smelled so wonderful, it couldn't possibly be nasty or make him ill.

He bit into the leaf. It was delicious! He knew it; it was a wonder plant – aromatic and tasty. He nibbled another leaf and another and another!

In the end he ate so many that the right side of the catnip plant looked like it had been ripped off.

Garfy looked around guiltily. He didn't want to ruin someone's garden or for the owners to think badly of him. Hoping no one had seen him, he trotted off down the road.

***

Now, one thing that happens to cats when they eat catnip is that, after a while, it can make them very sleepy. Garfy was no exception.

As soon as he began to walk he felt so tired he could hardly stand up straight.

"Oh my goodness, whatever will people think?" he thought.

A wave of exhaustion came over him. Although his legs felt like lead and too weak to carry him, he padded down the road away from the ruined plant and the possibility of being caught red-pawed.

"Maybe I could get to Paterson's," he thought. The idea of the soft bale of towels in the homeware aisle seemed dreamy but the reality was his legs wouldn't get him that far.

Garfy had never been so tired – not even when he was a kitten and chased everything that moved until he was exhausted, had he felt like this. Never had all four of his legs, his head, even his whiskers, felt like they were melting into the pavement.

He sighed with the effort of the walk. He might manage it to the corner shop and he could rest up there. Perhaps Vicki, the lady who ran the shop, would help him. She knew David and she knew where they lived, so perhaps she would carry him back to his nice warm bed.

When he got there, however, Garfy couldn't even raise his head to look in the shop window. Instead he eyed one of the cardboard boxes which had been put outside, ready for the bin men to come.

The box was greasy on two sides, like something had burst and leaked inside it. The top flaps were all bashed and broken and one of the edges had split as if it had been thrown from a great height.

To Garfy, so exhausted, it looked like a palace. He climbed in and before you could say Garfield Abercrombie Reginald Fergusson, he was curled up with his paws over his head and fast asleep.

***

A car pulled up outside the corner shop and, slowly and deliberately, out climbed a man with a shock of white hair and a handlebar moustache. He coughed loudly and smoothed down his tweed jacket. He slammed the door of the car and walked up to the cardboard box where Garfy hadn't stirred, despite the noise of the man's arrival.

"Humph!" he said, looking down at the contents of the box. "Feral cat!"

He tutted and peered closer into the dirty box.

As Garfy had collapsed into sleep, the grease from the box had smeared itself all over his coat and made his white bib grey. He was unrecognisable.

"I don't know where they come from but they breed like rabbits!" the man continued. "Absolutely horrendous, sleeping in a filthy box, in the middle of the street, in broad daylight, if you please!"

He began waving at the other occupant of the car. "Martha, come and look! Darned feral cat just lying here! What is society coming to if we allow cats to breed and roam the streets without so much as a collar on them? The wretched thing looks like it hasn't seen a good square meal in a while either."

That wasn't strictly true. As you know, Garfy does like his dinner and he never says no to a treat... or five... but the dirt did make him look very unloved.

Martha got out of the passenger seat of the car and tip-toed over to where the man with the handlebar moustache frowned at the box. "Oh, the poor thing! Whatever will we do? Oh, Derek, what a poor little fellow!"

"Now, Martha, gather yourself; don't get hysterical," Derek instructed. "There's a simple explanation: the cat is feral and that's that."

"That's *what*?" asked Martha. "You can't just leave him there – never had a home, never had an ounce of love, poor thing."

"Martha, if you say 'poor thing' once more..." warned Derek. "The cat is feral, I tell you. Nothing to be done except leave it to—"

"Don't even say it," Martha cried out. "No! Not another word. I'm phoning Sybil. She'll know what to do..."

Derek sighed and opened the door to the corner shop. "Well, are you coming in, now you've got out of the car?"

Martha waved him away, angry at him as she punched the keys on her phone.

***

The phone rang in the hall at number 40, St Mary's Street.

"Hello?" said the white-haired lady who answered.

"Sybil, it's Martha. You'll never guess. A poor cat in a box! Right here on the street. The little mite seems to have been living rough for some time. Derek says it's feral; I think he's been abandoned."

Sybil tapped her walking stick on the stone floor of the hall. "Oh, what a shame… Well, I simply wouldn't know what to do with it."

"Would you…? Could you…?" Martha began.

"No, my dear. I'm afraid I have six cats already. I couldn't look after another, especially if it needed nursing – on account of my knees, you know."

Sybil knew that Martha was worried so she tried to reassure her. "I'll telephone Prudence, she'll know what to do."

***

Sybil's daughter Prudence answered her phone at the first ring. "Prudence, it's Mum. There's a cat in a box. Derek thinks it's feral but Martha thinks it's abandoned. Will you go and see?"

Prudence smiled at her mother's request. "I'm going into Ely in a few minutes, I'll stop by and see we can do with it."

***

Prudence was a sensible kind of person, so before she set out for Ely she gathered up a few things, just in case.

From under the kitchen sink she got her green rubber gloves. From the cupboard under the stairs she got disinfectant. From the airing cupboard she got a clean but elderly orange and brown blanket. She set them all in the basket at the front of her bike and off she went to see what the fuss was all about.

***

"Oh, the poor thing!" she said when she bent over the box.

"I know. That's what I said. I said 'poor thing,' didn't I, Derek?" said Martha.

Derek tutted again and mumbled under his breath – something about missing the cricket for a dirty cat.

Prudence looked closer into the box and frowned. "Well, he's certainly dirty," she agreed.

Garfy snorted loudly in his sleep and the onlookers jumped back.

"He's calling out in pain. I think he's hurt," said Prudence. "I'll phone my friend Tanya. She's a nurse. She'll know what to do."

She dialled the number. "Tanya, it's Prue. There's a cat in a box. Derek thinks it's feral; Martha thinks it's abandoned; I think it's hurt. Will you come and see?"

***

Tanya packed a bag with bandages, antiseptic wipes and a bottle of water and rushed down to the corner shop. Despite having seen some nasty sights as a nurse – like rusty nails in hands and deep cuts in knees that had to be sewn back up – the sight of a filthy cat lying there all hurt made her gasp. A tear rolled down her cheek.

"How could anyone do such a thing to an innocent cat?" she said.

Prudence and Martha nodded their heads in agreement. All three leaned over the box which now housed Garfy. He hadn't so much as stirred, despite all the people crowded round him. The tatty brown and orange blanket had been laid carefully over him, which made him look even more destitute. The whole scene was a horrid mess.

Tanya stood back up quickly, which startled the others. She was quite stern when she looked at them. "This is cat abuse," she announced.

Martha and Prudence gasped. "Oh no! What are we going to do?" asked Martha.

"I know," Tanya replied. "I'll phone the cat shelter. They'll have the answer."

***

"Jenny, it's Tanya. There's a cat in a box. Derek thinks it's feral; Martha thinks it's abandoned; Prudence thinks it's hurt; I think it's cat abuse. Will you come and see?"

Now, Jenny knew all about the sad and horrible things that sometimes happen to all sorts of animals. She worked hard to prevent it happening so Tanya's phone call made her blood boil.

"Right! This needs *sorting*," she declared down the phone. "Leave it with me."

She looked around the reception of the cat shelter. There was no one else there. She couldn't abandon her post.

She filled out a report from the things that Tanya had told her: "Dirty ginger cat, in a box, feral, abandoned, injured, terrible case of cat abuse…" She shook her head in dismay. How could people do such a thing?

Then she phoned her friend Ameena at the *Ely Enquirer*. They simply *must* tell people about this awful case of cat abuse and do what they could to stop it from happening again.

***

Ameena quickly dispatched Gordon, the *Enquirer*'s photo-journalist, to find out what was going on and gather witness reports to write the story. It had been a quiet news week at the newspaper and this could make front-page news – "Cat abused and abandoned on Ely street!" Already she was composing the article from what Jenny had told her. She might even make it this week's editorial feature:

What has Ely come to, that this is how we treat our cats? She even remembered a quote about society being judged on how it treated its pets and began to hunt for who had said it.

***

Gordon was ready in two minutes and made a beeline to the corner shop. A crowd had started to gather by now and he had to say many an, "excuse me," to get through.

Martha, Prudence and Tanya were still there, creating a guard around the box. Derek had gone back to the car and had the radio up very loud, listening to the cricket. Every now and again he would look up at the swelling crowd and mutter to himself about feral cats.

Gordon pushed through the crowd. "What's the story, ladies?" he asked.

"Well," said Martha (she'd appointed herself spokesperson), "Derek saw the box as he was walking to the shop. He thinks it's feral; I thinks it's abandoned; Prudence thinks it's hurt; Tanya thinks it's cat abuse. Take a look."

Gordon glanced in. He'd made his mind up very quickly. What a dirty creature, greasy fur, all matted down one side; and was he right in thinking that the cat was hardly breathing? He looked harder. Yes, the cat had such a shallow breath, he thought the wretched creature was on his last legs. And what was that by the side of his mouth? It was slimy and green and seemed to have come from the cat itself.

"He's been poisoned!" Gordon exclaimed. The crowd gasped. Gordon took close-up shots of Garfy and the green slime.

In fact, it wasn't green slime. It was the disinfectant that Prudence had brought with her. She had squirted some around the sides of the box thinking it would clean the cat up a bit, wanting to make things better.

But it didn't make things better. It made no difference to Garfy, who was sound asleep, and it was making his current resting place look a whole lot worse. Slowly the green gel had slid down the sides of the box and oozed on to the base, right by Garfy's head.

"I'm calling the police," Gordon announced. This was very serious. He knew someone at the local police station. The police would know what to do.

Gordon pulled his phone out of his camera bag and dialled the number. He got through to the front desk. "This is Gordon from the *Ely Enquirer*. There's a cat in a box. Derek thinks it's feral; Martha thinks it's abandoned; Prudence thinks it's hurt; Tanya has reported cat abuse; I think it's been poisoned. Will you come?"

The police sent a squad car immediately. Poisoning was a serious business. They didn't want the whole of Ely to become ill. They had to move fast to stop it spreading and then the news going nationwide. The last thing they wanted was Ely being crammed with cameras and reporters, all commenting on how the poison had been introduced and telling the police how they ought to deal with it.

***

At the corner shop, the faint wail of sirens floated down the street and quickly became louder as the squad car swept down the road towards the shop. The crowd was growing all the time, as anyone who passed by stopped to see what was going on and to peer at the sleeping cat.

By now the green disinfectant had spread into the grease in the box and all over one side of Garfy's fur. The combination of rancid grease and disinfectant was giving off an awful smell.

***

PC Phil stepped out of his police car, walked purposefully towards the crowd and sniffed. His nose wrinkled when the smell of the grease and disinfectant reached his nostrils. Garfy was immersed in a very deep sleep with no idea what was going on around him. In his dreams he was sitting in his meadow, with flowers all around him.

The crowds surrounding the box were quiet, fearful of disturbing the feral/abandoned/injured/abused/poisoned cat.

Martha and Prudence were whispering while Tanya bent down trying to find Garfy's pulse.

PC Phil crouched down beside her but stood up again immediately. The smell was getting stronger. This alarmed Phil. It smelled serious.

He hastily retreated to his car, pulled on his high-vis jacket and unhooked the radio from its cradle.

"This is Sierra Bravo 472, responding to the report of poisoning in St. Catharine's Road.

"Suspect the area is contaminated. Dispatch fire brigade to assist. We need to cordon off the area."

***

The police call-handler dispatched a unit from the local fire station, with a quick history: "There's a cat in a box. Derek thinks it's feral; Martha thinks it's abandoned; Prudence thinks it's hurt; Tanya reported cat abuse; Gordon thinks it's poison; PC Phil thinks it's infected. Initiate emergency procedures and cordon off the area."

***

The gathered crowd was now so big that the box was completely hidden from the road. Children were trying to push past people's legs to get a good look. All around, people were craning their necks trying to see what was going on.

Martha looked very distressed. With all these people taking up air, how was the poor thing going to breathe?

How was anyone going to get through to help? Prudence patted her arm but even she was starting to feel worried.

There was a murmuring in the crowd. Someone said something about the cat being trapped in the box with a broken leg. Another heard this and told a neighbour that it was a fox. Someone else misheard *that* and decided it was probably a malformed offspring of a Fen tiger. It was like a game of Chinese Whispers with the story getting wilder and wilder at every telling.

***

When the fire engine screeched to a halt outside the corner shop, people scattered to allow the fire chief to climb down out of the cab.

She and PC Phil had a debrief. Everyone thought it was something. Everyone thought it was serious. Very serious…

"Hmm…" said the fire chief. She instructed the crew and they all jumped into action. *Operation outbreak* was go!

Phil went to his car and got out a large roll of tape and a megaphone. He entered the shop and instructed everyone to, "Please leave now as the area is being sealed off."

The shop customers were escorted off the premises and stood out on the road with the rest of the crowd. Bright orange bollards were placed, radiating out five metres from where the grubby box and blanket sheltered the slumbering Garfy.

All the roads in the area were closed off in both directions. More police arrived and started knocking on doors, telling people to close their windows and stay indoors to avoid contamination.

Everyone started to feel a little uneasy when a police helicopter flew overhead, dispatched to keep an eye on the situation from above. People in the crowds started to edge away but, to prevent the infection spreading, the police wouldn't let them leave. Anyone who had stopped to gawp at the unfortunate cat was now being told they were at risk of some terrible cat-borne disease (which, if you ask me, serves them right for being so nosey!).

As rumours spread about the infection and the possibility of quarantine, panic began to rise in the air. What was going to happen?

Martha, Prudence and Tanya had touched the cat so they would surely be raced away to hospital. They'd be in sealed-off rooms, no one would be able to visit. They'd have to be treated by doctors and nurses all in sealed suits and helmets with oxygen tanks on their backs.

"Maybe their skin will melt right off their faces," said Bobby to his school friends. They all sniggered at the thought.

His mum glared at him. "It's bad enough already. Don't make things worse. What if you are infected?" She immediately wished she hadn't said it. It really did make things worse.

People nearby overheard the last three words and became very alarmed and confused as they tried to get away from the child who, according to his mother, was showing signs of the deadly virus.

The noise was deafening, with everyone trying to leave, more police arriving to stop them, people shouting at Phil and the fire chief, and the helicopter rotor blades slicing the sky above.

***

Now, when Garfy first arrived at the corner shop, he hadn't managed to see his friend Vicki. After serving Derek, she'd gone out to the back of the shop, the security door closed and her head in the safe, counting the money ready for banking.

When she was done she stood up, shut the safe door and opened the heavy door which kept her office separate from the rest of the shop. Immediately she could hear panicked cries outside.

"What on earth?" She went through the empty shop to the front door. "Where did everyone come from?" she said to no one in particular. The door creaked loudly as she opened it and a hush came over the crowd. Vicki looked around, baffled at what had happened while she was working.

She stepped out and the crowd held its breath.

Martha called to her. "Be careful, Vicki, love! It's dangerous!" and she retold the story to Vicki.

"There's a cat in a box. Derek thinks it's feral; I think it's abandoned; Prudence thinks it's hurt; Tanya says it's cat abuse; Gordon thinks it's poison; the police think it's infected; the fire chief thinks we should all be in quarantine!"

Vicki was aghast. How could this happen to such a quiet corner of Ely? And so fast? It felt like something out of the movies.

As everyone stared at her, she inched towards the box and peeped in, cautiously. The smell was quite overpowering. What she saw was quite familiar though.

Vicki had meant to flatten this box earlier but had been distracted by a customer, so had left it on the pavement. It had been a damaged box and, earlier, she had spilled a bottle of sauce in it when the lid came off unexpectedly. She saw the bottle of disinfectant that Prudence had left there and, picking it up, began to laugh.

The crowd gasped. Was this woman crazy? Did she not understand? Or was this her evil plan to destroy the city? Perhaps this crazy laughing was the first symptom of the terrible disease which was sweeping the city. Or was she just horribly cruel – laughing at a poor dying cat?

***

As the whole of Ely looked on, Garfy moved from under the blanket, stood up, stretched and yawned, hopped out of the box and started off down the road to home.

"I'm starving," he thought. "What are all these people doing here? Haven't they got anything better to do?"

***

The cricket coverage on the radio had finished. Gordon, who had been paying no attention to what was going on outside, opened the car door and stepped out.

Suddenly he sneezed – three short, loud sneezes.

The crowd turned to him, then back to Phil and the fire chief, who had broken into a run, with bollards and tape in their hands.

4

Garfy Framed

Have you ever noticed how everybody loves a celebrity? Then, as they get more famous, some people start looking for ways to say something nasty about them or prove that they aren't perfect?

I don't know about you but I've always wondered why these people act that way.

***

Garfy was certainly a celebrity and he was quite used to media attention. So, when the whole of Ely got terribly excited about the whole incident of 'the cat in a box' and the fuss that had been made, the elegant ginger tom took it all in his stride.

For the whole of the following week, after he had almost caused a mass evacuation of the city, David's phone was ringing constantly as he reassured the papers and the local television news that Garfy was perfectly healthy and it had all been a misunderstanding.

***

As David drew back the curtain at the weekend, he was dismayed to see one reporter still outside the house taking pictures and waiting for an exclusive interview.

"I don't know, Garfy," he said with a sigh, "trouble certainly knows where you live. It's always finding you." Then he shrugged at the sight of the scruffy fellow standing out there in the rain. "It must be a slow news week. If he wants to waste his time trying to find a story where there isn't one, that's his lookout," and he closed the curtain again.

***

Garfy secretly liked being the centre of attention. "You can't be a celebrity cat without the media," he thought but even he was starting to worry that things had gone a little too far this time. He had been looking forward to his morning trip down to Paterson's – Saturday was always his favourite morning because so many people were there to greet him. Now though, he wasn't sure he would go. He really didn't want to go out and face that reporter. No good would come of it, he was sure.

***

Outside Garfy's house stood investigative journalist Eddie Jackford. He had been dispatched by Ameena from the *Ely Enquirer* to cover the after-effects of the suspected infection of St. Catharine's Road.

Ameena had been delighted with the article Eddie wrote and printed it on the front page.

Now Eddie wanted more of his stories on the front page. He was new to Ely and wanted to prove himself. He wanted to show that he could get a 'scoop' – a story so huge and exciting that it would make national news and get him a job on one of the big newspapers.

He was sure there was more to be unearthed about this cat who so interested everyone in Ely and the surrounding area.

Determined to make his name, Eddie didn't care about the weather.

***

Outside he stayed, until Garfy couldn't bear it any longer and he simply had to get some fresh air. Maybe, if he was very quiet, he might be able to sneak away and get to Paterson's without the reporter knowing.

No such luck!

No matter how careful he was, no matter how much stealth he could muster, Garfy was always noticed by someone. He managed to get to the corner without the reporter looking up from his phone but then Jack and Megan, who lived two doors down, came out of their house.

"Morning, Garfy. Off somewhere nice?" they called. "Looking for a nice clean box this time, eh?" They laughed as they walked on.

Garfy flattened his ears. Would he ever live this down? It wasn't as if he'd even been awake when everyone got so excited. Humans were so strange the way they made a fuss.

Eddie Jackford looked up from his phone when he heard the voices. He hadn't heard the front door or a cat trying to sneak away but was delighted to be able to catch the ginger tom.

"Ah! Garfy, can I stop you for a minute? I just want to ask you a few questions. I'm a big fan," he added with an oily grin in his face.

Garfy was tempted. He enjoyed the limelight and he loved looking at his photograph in the papers. But he remembered his thoughts of earlier – *no good will come of it* – so he quickened his pace and ran across the road.

That didn't stop Eddie. He began to run in pursuit.

Garfy leapt over the curb onto the pavement and began sprinting towards Paterson's. He darted down the side of the building but the reporter was hot on his heels, calling to him.

"It won't take long, Garfy, I just want two minutes of your time."

Garfy dashed into the foyer of Paterson's and around the corner to the aisles. He raced down through the fruit and veg aisle, narrowly avoiding a huge trolley laden with watermelons. Then he was into the pizza and ready-meal aisle, motoring towards the deli counter.

Eddie was used to running too and nothing stopped him when he smelled a story so he was close on the heels of the agile cat.

Suddenly, just as he was about to run straight into the glass of the deli counter, Garfy changed direction, ran past the homeware department and his favourite spot on the towels and then doubled back towards the foyer.

Paterson's back-to-school range was being taken down and there were wheeled cages and piles of clothes everywhere on the floor.

Garfy skidded round the end where all the fluffy pencil cases were being thrown into a basket and dashed under a huge stock of girls' grey skirts.

***

Eddie still had sight of the fleeing cat until they came back towards the foyer but the newspaper racks briefly caught his eye and he paused to look at the headlines.

They all had enticing titles to make people want to buy them:

"Man accused of stealing a bread roll from the Prime Minister."

"Storm heading towards the UK."

Most interesting to Eddie was, "Celebrity's reputation in ruins after shocking story revealed."

Very interesting indeed! Could this be the answer?

Eddie knew that Garfy was *the* local celebrity, had his portrait in the Paterson's foyer and had become famous far beyond Ely. He'd even had a book written about him!

Perhaps, if he read through all the old articles about the elegant ginger cat he might find something that would question Garfy's reputation. That sold newspapers and got you noticed as a reporter.

He abandoned the chase and walked back to the *Ely Enquirer's* offices to get down to some serious research. This could be the article that would set him up for a career at a big newspaper.

"No more writing about cake sales and horses getting stuck in fields," he muttered to himself as he left Paterson's.

***

That afternoon, Eddie sat at his computer going through all the old articles about Garfy's adventures.

The first one he came across was the opening of Paterson's. Garfy had been there at the beginning, supervising the building of the superstore and was their resident cat. When it opened, however, he had upstaged the very important person who had come to officially open it and, at the same time, upset Mr Bennet, the store manager.

Could he write about that? Garfy as an identity thief? No, it didn't quite fit. Besides, he had had a run-in with Josh Batt himself when he'd written an article saying that the councillor wasn't good at his job. There was no way Batt would help him.

Garfy, Identity Thief wasn't sensational enough. He had to look further.

***

Next Eddie found a tiny article about Garfy coming to visit Paterson's nearly every day since it had opened. It went on to tell a story about how he befriended everyone at the superstore and how he was very often given treats by the shoppers. "Nothing sensational so far," sighed Eddie. The story ended with the funny story of when Garfy had managed to get all the way into the café without anyone noticing and pinched Mr Bennet's tuna sandwich.

Was this it? Garfy the thief?

It proved how the ginger tom would stop at nothing to get what he wanted.

***

Just before Paterson's closed that evening, Eddie rushed down to see if he could get an interview with Mr Bennet. It was the store manager's sandwich so his point of view would give depth to the article. It was well-known that there was no love lost between Mr Bennet and Garfy.

Showing the poor, hardworking victim and his suffering would help make the story successful enough for Eddie to get noticed by the national newspapers.

"Cover all the bases," he thought.

"Mr Bennet," said one of Paterson's assistants over the phone, "there's a Mr Jackford at customer services. He says he wants to talk to you about an incident that happened between you and Garfy, over a tuna sandwich."

Mr Bennet could hear sniggering in the background. He remembered that day all too well. He had chased the thieving cat through the store and ended up skidding over spilled washing-up liquid and landing flat on his back! He shuddered just thinking about it.

What did this Jackford want, bringing all this back up again?

No, he tried to stay well clear of that cat. He knew that he couldn't get rid of him.

Garfy was an attraction who brought more shoppers to the superstore than any other Paterson's in the country. He was well-loved to this day and nothing Mr Bennet ever did to try and stop him ever ended well.

"Tell Mr Jackford that I have no comment." With that, he slammed down the phone and packed his briefcase.

Hearing the news that Mr Bennet wouldn't speak to him, Eddie slunk off home.

***

By the next day, Eddie was back at the *Ely Enquirer* scrolling through articles again and he was much cheered by what he found. He thought he'd found the perfect story.

He had uncovered a letter written to the paper, from someone called Sebastian Harding, a dog-lover and regular contributor to the letters section. Sebastian had written complaining about the violence of cats. He had blamed the owners and their failure to teach their cats how to behave. Dog owners were much more responsible, he had written.

His opinion was that cat owners were allowing their pets to ruin other people's gardens, yowl at all times of the night and, worst of all, fight with each other.

Was Garfy part of this? Eddie could see the headlines now – *Ginger tom is local gang leader.* Eddie could write that Garfy was responsible for causing havoc up and down the city, recruiting young kittens to his violent gang and turning them into cold-blooded attack-cats.

***

The next article Eddie found backed the 'violent' theory up nicely. Garfy had been in a fight and that had triggered an interest in body-building. With the help of a gym owner, he became fit and strong and had seen off the other cat, a big black called Tyson.

There it was in black and white! Garfy and Tyson were gang leaders, fighting over their 'turf', carving up the city between them, battling over every street and every new kitten that was born.

This story would stick, Eddie felt sure.

All he needed was an interview – one with someone who had knowledge of the story and knew both cats.

***

Eddie left the office and strode up to the city centre, full of excitement. Who could he ask? He glanced into shop windows as he passed. They all seemed to have the same poster in their windows.

"Equality for all animals," they all declared.

The poster was promoting the mayor's next initiative to create zones all around the city and inside the shops. There, pets could relax, warm and comfortable, instead of being tied up outside while their owners shopped. It was for all kinds of animals too – dogs and cats alike – and if someone wanted to bring their gerbil along, that was also fine.

How was the ambitious reporter going to get a sensational story about Ely's best-loved cat if this was happening? (He did wonder briefly how bringing gerbils to the pet zones would work. After all, a pet gerbil must look like a plaything to your average cat. Perhaps there was a story in that…)

Eddie was beginning to think that all of Ely was completely batty, when he turned to see Colonel Oakeshott coming towards him, with his wife alongside him. The Colonel might be a good bet to spill the beans on something Garfy had done.

"Ah, yes, Garfy…" Colonel Oakeshott mused. "Daft as a brush, that one! Always getting into scrapes, the clumsy oaf."

This sounded promising. Eddie pressed him for more.

The Colonel cleared his throat. "Harrumph. Always thought he was trouble, skulking about and making a nuisance of himself, sleeping in dirty boxes in the middle of the street. Wouldn't be surprised if he was savage with it."

Eddie smiled. This *was* a story! He would be famous, he'd get the scoop of the century! "Oh no!" said his wife. "That poor thing! He's a lovely friendly fellow. He's no more savage than my Aunt Mabel." She frowned at the journalist. "Sorry, dear. You're barking up the wrong tree. Garfy has had some run-ins in the past but he isn't violent."

Eddie was beginning to feel very frustrated. Was there nothing that would stick? He thanked the couple as they turned towards the café on the corner.

"Did you hear what I said, Gerald?" he heard Mrs Oakeshott saying as he walked away. "*Barking up the wrong tree*. Do you get it?"

"Cats don't bark, Barbara," the Colonel said, shaking his head.

***

Everyone else he spoke to told Eddie what a lovely cat Garfy was.

Elegant and proud, yes, but a violent gang member? No.

Garfy cheered everyone up as soon as they saw him.

Eddie was back to square one. Maybe he should think about some other way to get his big scoop for the national papers. Even the story about Garfy getting above himself that one time wasn't worth writing about. After all, the cat had learned his lesson very quickly when all his friends got fed up with his snootiness and stopped visiting him at Paterson's. Friends were more important than anything else to Garfy. So, that story was no good.

What to do? What to write about?

***

Back at the *Ely Enquirer*, Eddie felt defeated. He sat with his head propped up on his hand while he scrolled up and down all the articles he had read about Garfy. There was nothing here. He would simply have to think of something else.

Just then, an idea came out from nowhere and hit him straight in the middle of his eyes! There was one story – something about cars – which was nudging at the back of his mind.

Garfy had always been fascinated with cars and liked getting into them as often as the drivers would let him. Eddie had already heard lots of tales of how the ginger tom was often found curled up on the back seat or standing in the driver's seat looking through the windscreen and leaning on the steering wheel, as if he wanted to drive away.

As Eddie pondered this, an idea started to form and became clearer and clearer. Paterson's… cars… trips to the seaside…

"That's it!" Eddie shouted, out loud, making everyone else in the newsroom stare at him. "Garfy is a smuggler!"

All that time spent befriending everyone in Paterson's was so he could steal goods from the shop. Then he would stash the contraband in the cars, so he could take them to the seaside and get them on boats to other countries, illegally. Then, some partner of his at the coast would get goods from boats, load them back into the cars (probably using that same 'adorable' trick of hopping into cars). That would get them back to Ely where Garfy would supervise their distribution across the country!

**

Eddie set to work. This would be his greatest story yet. He came across a news report of Garfy spending several days at the coast with some local cat. They must have been running their smuggling business for years. The other cat had even made it to Ely once, to visit Garfy.

Eddie began to build a story around the scant facts he had. He invented a thriving business, needing two cats, or more, to oversee the operations. He knew he could weave in the gang element too, to give the story strength and conviction.

His article began to shape up. It started with the innocent people of Ely being duped by their favourite cat, Garfield Abercrombie Reginald Fergusson, no less. It went on about how the supposed 'elegant and smart' ginger cat had been running a smuggling racket for years.

Then he explained the theory about the reason behind the car-hopping and coastal trips, expanding this with the idea of a network of gang-cats who were spreading the contraband all across the nation.

***

It sounded a little fanciful but Eddie knew that newspapers sold millions of copies with articles just like this. Even if it proved not to be true, who was going to make an issue about printing lies about a *cat*? It wasn't as if Garfy could sue the paper.

***

Writing the article took several days as Eddie tracked down people who could back up the story. Some shoppers told him that Garfy indeed got into their cars. Others said that Garfy would raid their shopping bags to see what was in them. It was said with love and amusement. Garfy was just being a cheeky cat or curious to explore. Not one person suggested any evil intent or that Garfy was a mastermind smuggling gang leader.

That was the twist Eddie put on it, however. Garfy's reputation would be under the microscope and everyone would know that he, Eddie, was a top investigative journalist.

***

Late into the night, as Eddie was finishing up the article, he dreamed of the reaction when he sent it to the *Daily Tale*, the country's biggest-selling newspaper.

He was so absorbed that he didn't see Ameena standing behind him, reading over his shoulder.

"Wow, Eddie! This is your best work yet! Let's get it on the front page for tomorrow's news."

If only he'd been more careful! Ameena had discovered that he was writing an exposé, unaware that it was destined for 'the nationals.' Now, all that effort was for nothing. He had to submit it to the *Ely Enquirer* instead.

What a waste! He would have to think of something else to get him more widespread attention.

***

Sales of the *Ely Enquirer* soared through the roof. They had to do two extra print runs. Everyone was talking about Garfy and his secret life.

David was mortified and so were the people who had talked to the reporter. They thought Eddie was writing a nice piece about Garfy and his funny ways. Now, they discovered, all he wanted to do was make up some sensational story to sell more newspapers.

Every day, for the next week, Eddie came up with another side to the story to further damage Garfy's reputation.

Not many people truly believed it but they couldn't help buying the paper to find out what else he was supposed to have done.

***

Garfy couldn't believe the lies that were being told about him and how quickly people turned on him. He went to

Paterson's less and less for fear of being jeered at until, one day, he stopped going altogether.

David tried to comfort him. "It will all blow over, Garfy. People will forget soon enough. Don't worry, I'm sure something will turn up to show that you aren't this master-villain the *Enquirer* is saying you are."

It was hard though. David tried to find the lorry driver who had unknowingly taken the ginger tom to the seaside that day, so she could tell everyone it was all a terrible mistake – but it was like looking for a needle in a haystack.

Jenny, who had found Garfy at the seaside, couldn't help to clear Garfy's name either. She told the newspaper that it was all lies but they just kept churning out story after story about gangs and stolen goods and mysterious disappearances.

***

Poor Garfy! He wasn't sleeping, he wasn't eating and he jumped every time someone knocked at the door. The articles were getting more and more critical of 'Ely's most famous cat' and there was very little anyone could do to get at the truth.

Then, just when it seemed that Garfy's darkest hour had come… it got worse.

***

Late one morning, there came a loud knock at the door. Garfy had managed to swallow down a morsel of tuna and was curled up in his bed, when David showed in two police officers.

They looked down at Garfy who leapt up and stood to attention, not knowing what to do with himself. He tried to look innocent – his eyes were downcast, his ears were flat against his head and his tail was motionless.

One policeman was talking in a loud whisper. "We have no option," Garfy heard him say.

The other police officer bent down and said, in a sorrowful tone, "Garfield Abercrombie Reginald Fergusson, I am arresting you on suspicion of running a smuggling ring. You do not have to say anything but it may harm your defence if you do not mention, when questioned, something which you later rely on in court. Anything you do say may be given in evidence."

She began to take the handcuffs out of their holder on her belt but then thought better of it. How would Garfy walk to the car with great big handcuffs around his legs? They put him in his cat box instead and used the handcuffs to secure it.

Garfy yowled for David. He couldn't believe this was happening.

"Don't worry. I'll get help. We'll find a way, Garfy!" David called as the police car drove away.

***

At the police station Garfy was led to the front desk.

The sergeant on duty didn't look up from his computer. "Name?"

"Garfield Abercrombie Reginald Fergusson," said the arresting police officer.

"Reason for arrest?"

"Suspicion of smuggling," came the reply.

This got the sergeant's attention. He looked at the two police officers then around him. He couldn't see who had been arrested. One of the police officers picked up the cat box and showed the sergeant who was inside.

"Hello, Garfy! What are... Oh." He couldn't believe this. Arresting a cat! They had good grounds though and no one had stepped forward yet to prove Garfy was innocent.

The sergeant picked Garfy out of his cat box, set him down on the desk and got out a large ink stamp.

Garfy was used to this! Did the sergeant want his signature? He had signed so many books before and wondered if this was all just an elaborate joke so he could do a book signing for the police.

Unfortunately not. Garfy was being 'processed'.

He had his paw prints recorded and a 'mug shot' photograph taken. He was even searched!

Most undignified! What were they going to find in a cat's fur? Fleas?

"Not on this cat!" thought Garfy.

***

Once he'd been interviewed for what seemed like hours, Garfy was led to a cell and locked in for the night.

With his head hung low and his tail drooping on the floor, Garfy moaned softly to himself.

How could anyone think he was a smuggler – a gang leader?

***

Out around the city, the papers ran the front-page story of Garfy's arrest. He was the talk of the town yet again but this time for all the wrong reasons.

The *Ely Enquirer* – first to break the story – was selling in the tens of thousands but Eddie still wasn't satisfied. He couldn't believe he'd been so stupid as to get caught writing the story and then have to hand it over to local news. He'd had the chance to write some really sensational stuff though, so he would just keep on practising, waiting for another scoop to sell to the *Daily Tale*.

***

Back at the police station, the police officers were getting more and more confused about the whole business. Witnesses were being interviewed in their dozens, all telling their stories about Garfy and all of them seemed to be conflicting. Nothing matched up.

The investigating officer had no choice but to apply to hold Garfy for longer.

***

Days went by and David was running out of ideas.

He had talked again to Jenny about what had happened when she found him at the beach and the other cat who had been with him.

Neither of them knew how to get hold of Salty any more. She'd had to move out of her old broken boat in the middle of the crazy golf course. The council were ripping it down to build luxury apartments on the seafront and no one knew where the coastal cat had gone.

The police still couldn't find the driver who had taken Garfy there either and they suspected her of being part of the whole sorry business.

Every piece of evidence, every story, hinged on why Garfy was at the seaside. A police officer had been stationed at Paterson's for two days, waiting to see if the driver would deliver there again.

The news spread like wildfire. Papers in other counties began to run the story and it finally got to the very same coastal town where Garfy was supposed to be running his smuggling operation.

***

That evening, Salty went to the promenade to see if anyone had left anything from a fish and chip supper on any of the benches. The bench closest to the new luxury flats had a morsel or two and, with it, an abandoned newspaper.

Salty read as she nibbled on the scraps of fish but then sat bolt upright. What she saw almost made her spit her food straight out of her mouth!

Garfy was in trouble again and this time it was deep trouble.

Salty knew she had to help and that there was no time to lose. All the lorries departed from the fish-processing warehouse at the end of the promenade. She had to get to the right one – and quick.

***

As she rounded the corner beyond which the warehouse stood, she saw the Ely lorry leaving and the large gates closing behind it. Salty was too late!

Already the lorry was picking up speed. Salty was well behind it and soon it would reach the main road and be gone. However fast she ran, she'd never catch it.

Suddenly, the lorry stopped, just before the roundabout to the main road. The door on the back was rattling and the driver had pulled up to investigate. She climbed out of her cab to see what the noise was.

This was Salty's chance! She sprinted towards the open cab door and, just as she leapt in and hid herself under a large duffel bag, the driver got back in and started up the engine.

Paws crossed she'd picked the right lorry.

***

It seemed an age before the lorry stopped and the driver got back out. She was opening the back door again. Salty sneaked a quick look out of the window, hoping nobody would see her. The sight that met her eyes filled her with relief. She was at the loading bay of Paterson's Superstore! Now, if she remembered rightly, Garfy's house was only across the road and up a bit.

Stealthily, Salty crept down the steps of the cab and under the lorry. When the coast was clear, she made a dash for the road and was across it in a few bounds. But she hadn't gone unnoticed.

The driver saw Salty jump down from her lorry and began running after her, thinking she'd stolen something.

***

When David saw Salty standing at the window, it gave him such a fright! He couldn't believe she was here.

What gave him more of a fright was the lorry driver, Lucy, staring at him too!

What a bonus! Now Garfy could be cleared.

Lucy looked cross but David quickly started to explain everything to her.

Lucy couldn't keep up. What were they doing arresting an innocent cat? She, in turn, told David what she remembered from the day Garfy had found himself at the coast. She'd seen him jump down from the cab but only from a distance and then couldn't find him anywhere.

Because she didn't know how he'd come to be in her cab or where he lived, she couldn't tell anyone. She'd found cat hair in her bed and concluded that Garfy got in, fell asleep and accidentally hitched a lift all the way to the seaside!

David beamed. This was just what the police needed to hear. "You are a lifesaver," he said.

***

Together they hurried down to the police station where Lucy retold her story. Everything slotted into place.

The police were satisfied that Garfy could be cleared of all charges.

"Nice to have had you at our station," said the sergeant as he escorted Garfy out of the cells. "What an elegant cat you are."

***

Eddie was outside the station, waiting. "Any words for the front page? How do you feel about this miscarriage of justice? What does this say about modern policing?" he asked, hunting for a new story now that the sensation of Garfy as a criminal had been proven untrue.

David and the Lucy ignored him. It's the only thing you can do.

***

The paper ran one last story on the whole caper, exonerating Garfy completely. It sold the most copies ever in the history of the *Ely Enquirer*.

And the future of Eddie's career?

The *Daily Tale* had seen the stories about Garfy, but they still weren't sensational enough for their front page. Eddie would have to come up with something even more extraordinary to win them over.

***

Back at the office, Ameena said, "Great work these past few days. I've got a real scoop for you this time. Two horses stuck in mud."

***

David invited the Lucy back to the house for a bite to eat. Garfy was over the moon to see Salty and, as David prepared food, Salty told him all about moving to a new place.

"It's perfect," she said. "A little dinghy in a shed, right next to the bins at the back of the fish warehouse. Free food, all day, every day."

And for their supper?

Well, fish and chips of course!

5

Biblio-Cat

Garfield Abercrombie Reginald Fergusson eased his way out of his cat flap and stretched down on to his front paws, so that his smart stripes smoothed all the way down. He breathed in deeply, smelling the beautiful rose sitting in the pot next to the front door. It was a cutting from the one that grew over Kenji and Hana's tea house and the scent of the rose reminded Garfy of all the friends he had in Ely – so many that he'd lost count.

***

Today was going to be a good day. He was going to visit Sam, one of his favourite friends at Paterson's. Sam was one of the floor managers there and had been there from the day the superstore had opened. Garfy and Sam had been fast friends ever since and they always enjoyed a cup of tea and a tin of sardines together when it was a slow day at Paterson's.

Sam loved books and would often read to Garfy on his lunch break. He very much liked Garfy's biography, which had been written the year before and he even had a signed copy from the author. He loved the look of books, he loved the words in books, he even loved the smell of books.

"One day," he would tell Garfy, "I'm going to have a bookshop of my own, so I can spend all day reading!"

***

As Garfy looked out on to the world from his front garden, he hoped that today was going to be a slow day at Paterson's, so he could spend time with Sam and have time for a sardine or two and a cuppa. Garfy was particularly hungry, so he prayed for a big tin of fish.

He trotted across the road and down to the foyer of the superstore. There was Sam, pacing up and down as if he had something very serious on his mind. When he saw Garfy, however, his serious face was transformed with the beaming smile.

"Garfy! I'm so glad you made it. I have something exciting to tell you!" With that, he ran back to his office so fast that Garfy found it hard to keep up.

When he got there, a corner of his desk was laid with a tablecloth, two cups and a teapot – but no tin of fish.

Garfy was a trifle disappointed. Of course, he came to see his friend Sam but the sardines made the visit even more pleasurable.

"Never mind," he said to himself, "a cuppa will do nicely."

Sam had his back to Garfy with his face in the cupboard and when he turned around, he had the biggest cake in his hand that Garfy had ever seen.

"It's sardine cake!" Sam beamed. "I've got something to celebrate!"

As he set the cake down on the desk, Sam said, "You know the bookshop on the High Street? Well, old Mr Robinson is retiring and he's selling the business!" He grinned. "Garfy, I'm leaving Paterson's and I'm buying the Robinson's bookshop!"

Garfy didn't know whether to laugh or cry. He was so pleased for Sam. This is what his friend had always wanted to do – to own his own bookshop.

On the other hand, he was going to miss seeing Sam at Paterson's. He was certainly going to miss listening to passages from his favourite books as he nibbled on sardines and sipped tea. It was all so dignified. Who was he going to share a tin of fish with now?

"You never know," thought Garfy optimistically, "perhaps there's more chance of sardines at the bookshop with Sam in charge, than there is at Paterson's, having to dodge Mr Bennet all the time!"

***

Robinson's had been the biggest bookshop on Ely High Street ever since anyone could remember. No one ever remembered what was there before.

Maybe it had always been there. Maybe generations and generations of Robinson's had categorised and stacked and sold books as far back as the first printing machine.

It was a *very* old place.

People still visited, although they didn't always make a special trip to go there to buy their books like they did when Sam was a boy. This was especially so now supermarkets sold them and shoppers could buy books along with their groceries.

***

"It's a dream come true, Garfy!" Sam said, as he cut the cake. He raised his teacup. "Here's to my new bookshop business and many hours spent eating sardines and reading books!"

Garfy raised his chin to the ceiling. "Miaow!" he said in celebration.

***

Sam's last day at Paterson's came round very quickly and on his last day he packed up his desk as a small party went on around him. Everyone had brought some food to share.

Eileen had brought sausage rolls, August had brought neat little lemon cakes and Evan had brought a big box of homemade biscuits. Evan had gone back to college and was learning to be a baker. He was so good at it and was so inspired by Sam that he was going to start his own business as well, making and selling special biscuits.

"Good for you!" said Sam, biting into one of the ginger snaps. Delicious!

Garfy had, of course, brought a tin of sardines!

Sam was so pleased to see everyone. They were really going to miss him. He had been a great floor manager, always ready to help and lend a listening ear. He had a keen eye for detail and his section of Paterson's was always neat, tidy and welcoming.

He was going to miss Paterson's and all his friends but he knew they would all visit and spend some time (and a bit of money!) in his bookshop.

***

The next week, Sam took over Robinson's and became the official owner of a very old and, as Sam quickly discovered, very dusty, bookshop.

Garfy continued his daily visits to Paterson's. He still liked to have a nap on his bale of towels in the homeware aisle. It felt very different without Sam, though.

"Don't worry, Garfy," said Evan, when he saw the ginger tom moping around one day. "Sam has been hard at work cleaning, tidying and painting, and he's having a grand opening on Saturday, so you can go and see him then."

That did make Garfy feel a bit better. He would be able to see Sam and maybe have a sardine and a cuppa with him. He might even find a nice little spot in the sun to have a little snooze.

***

On Saturday Garfy was up bright and early, ready to visit Sam and his bookshop. He made sure his bib and socks were the whitest white and his stripes were smart and in line.

"Perfectly dignified," he thought as he looked in the mirror.

Now, how to get to the bookshop?

***

The problem with humans is that they don't always understand what cats are saying, so sometimes it was difficult for Garfy to ask for directions. He would have to find help some other way.

As he stepped out into the front garden deciding which way to go, Joan, his next-door neighbour, emerged at the same time.

"Hello, Garfy. Are you off to see Sam today? I hear he has his grand opening." She bent down to scratch him under the chin. "You'd better hop on the bus. It looks like it's going to rain. You don't want to get wet, when you look so smart."

Garfy looked up expectantly at her. "No, I can't give you a lift, I'm afraid. I have to work. We've got a big project on and I have lots to do to get it finished."

Off she went, pointing to the bus stop down the road. "Get the number 46," she called.

***

Garfy trotted down the road and joined the queue at the bus stop. It had started to rain, so the agile cat dashed quickly under the shelter, so as not to spoil the line of his stripes down his back.

All the humans were wearing raincoats and boots and some had waterproof hats on. They could tell from the grey skies overhead that it was going to tip it down for the whole morning.

Garfy couldn't understand the obsession humans had with covering every bit of their bodies with drab plastic clothing. Surely their fur would keep the rain off, like his did? He did see two sets of very colourful wellies though, tapping a little puddle that had gathered under a drip from the bus stop roof.

It was Drayden and Wesley who were waiting with their mother. They were so pleased to see Garfy that they snuck out of the queue to stroke him. "Hello, Garfy," they said together. "Are you going to see Sam today? Mum says we might be able to pop in when we've had our eyes tested."

Just then, the bus arrived and Drayden gathered Garfy in his arms and half-covered him with his coat. They stepped on.

Roma, the driver, was handing tickets to the passengers, so she saw Drayden get on, with a very curious-looking lump in his coat. She pretended not to notice the ginger tail poking out at the bottom. She winked at Drayden and whispered to his coat, "Hello, Garfy."

***

Now, as you know, Garfy loves riding in cars but he had never ridden in a bus before. What a treat it was!

He climbed out of Drayden's jacket and sat on Wesley's lap, looking out of the window. It was so high up. He could see everything going by: all the cars, all the people on the street heading into the market and all the shops which were lining the streets.

It was raining hard now and Garfy was so glad he was inside, steadily heading up the hill. He loved watching when the bus stopped as people got in and out each time. The bus was quite full now and it was very noisy.

As they came past the cathedral, Drayden and Wesley stood up with their mum.

"This is our stop," they said. "If you get off at the next stop, it's the nearest to Robinson's bookshop."

They left Garfy sitting alone on the seat, watching them skip down the street to the optician's. "I wonder what it means to *have your eyes tested*?" he thought. "Is it like the exams the children tell me about? Do the eyes answer questions together? Or separately?" He would never quite understand humans and their world.

***

The next stop came up quicker than Garfy expected and he jumped down from the seat just as a bottom was about to sit down on it. He weaved in and out of people's legs, under a pram and over the stick of an old man who was talking to Roma as she scanned his ticket.

The doors were shutting but Garfy took a leap at the opening and landed (elegantly of course) on the pavement outside. He was at one end of the high street and, as he looked along its length, he saw crowds of people in every direction.

It was market day and the humans were everywhere, with baskets and bikes and buggies, all full of meat from the butcher, bags of pasta and beans from the wholefood shop, and fruit and veg from the market stalls. There were armfuls of flowers and bread and cakes and sausages.

What a delight to Garfy's senses. Nearly as good as catnip!

The rain had eased to a drizzle and he trotted the full length of the street watching all the people come and go, in and out of shops.

***

Garfy had become so distracted by the sights and sounds and smells of Ely city centre, that he almost forgot why he was there.

"Right! Robinson's, where is Robinson's?" he reminded himself. He looked about but couldn't see it.

People's legs were getting in the way and he couldn't see the shop windows so he decided to go back to the very top of the street and work his way down all over again.

The rain had finally stopped and Garfy shook the rest of the drops off his fur. He strutted down the pavement, his head to the right, craning to see what the windows could tell him about the contents of the shops. "Clothes and handbags, no. Sandwiches and drinks, no. Shoes, no." He got to the middle of the street and still no sign of books anywhere.

He tried not to get distracted again but now the crowds had thinned a bit and people had started to notice the handsome feline walking around.

"Hello, Garfy!", "Hi, Garfy!" they called.

Most stopped to stroke his head or tickle him under his chin; some children even enticed him to sit on a bench next to them and share their snack.

It was all very pleasant but Garfy *had* to get to Robinson's. It was getting late, he could tell, by the rumbling of his stomach. So, polite though he was, Garfy made off quickly, trying to avoid legs and hands and tidbits held out to him.

***

Just as he was reaching the end of the street again, he saw what he'd been looking for. Garfy had walked right past the bookshop earlier but, because of the crowds and not being tall enough to quite see in the window, he had missed it.

There it was, with a grey-framed glass door and a big window with *Robinson's – Booksellers* written across the top. It was hardly a surprise he had almost missed it. The window was a little cloudy and it was hard to see exactly what was on display.

Sam was right. It was *very* dusty.

Garfy sighed with relief. He went inside and immediately made a little old lady squeal.

"Oh! My goodness. Mr Sam, Mr Sam!" she shouted, and in a quieter voice, almost a whisper, she said, "First it's mice, now it's cats. This place is more like a zoo than a bookshop."

She stood on tip-toes, clutching her chest until, around the long bookshelf in the middle, came Sam.

"What is it, Mrs Muldoon?" he began.

Garfy was so pleased to see him, he bounded up to him in two leaps and made the lady squeal again.

"Garfy! You came!" Sam said, picking him up and cuddling him. "Welcome to my bookshop!"

***

Garfy couldn't believe what he was seeing.

Books!

Not just on shelves and bookcases but on the floor, on the windowsills, stacked up higher than a human's head…

He wouldn't have been surprised if the walls were made out of books. It wasn't exactly a mess but it was certainly overcrowded.

The building which housed Robinson's was very old, narrow and tall, and the bookshop carried on for three floors. It had even spilled outside into a shed at the back and into the toilet on the second floor. Hundreds of thousands of books for adults and children alike. Garfy wondered if there were any for cats!

"It's my dream come true," Sam told him, "but it's hard work, my friend."

***

Sam led Garfy to a back room where he had set up a rickety old desk, piled high with books (of course!) and papers. On the corner, he had set out the usual tablecloth, teapot and cups, and a plate of sardines.

This room was very dusty too and there was a scratching, nibbling sound in the corner that was familiar to Garfy.

"It's not exactly the Ritz but the sardines are fresh," said Sam. He looked tired. "I haven't been able to sit and read all day yet – there is so much to do. Mrs Muldoon is trying to help but she's a little unsteady on her feet and she keeps knocking over the stacks of books with her broom."

Sam went on to tell his feline friend that he had been working very long days to get the bookshop smart, clean and tidy. It was a big job – bigger than he had expected and, to top it all, a huge extended family of mice lived here and were nibbling at the books faster than Sam or Mrs Muldoon could move them into newly built shelves. It was an uphill battle.

When Garfy followed Sam to the back room he noticed that the shop was also quiet. Apart from Mrs Muldoon, there were only about two or three people in the shop.

Sam could sense his disappointment, for he felt it also. "Not exactly the grand opening, is it, Garfy?" he sighed.

He cheered up a little though. It was so nice to have a friend to share a cuppa with. "Let me show you round," he said.

***

They started on the top floor. "Gardening and cooking this end, art and design the other." There was a little reading nook right next to a teetering pile of Timmy Welch's books.

"That looks like a nice place to have a snooze," thought Garfy. It had a plump blue pillow propped up against the side, a rug on the floor and a blanket on the bench, just in case anyone felt the urge to take off their shoes, curl up and get cosy.

The middle floor housed maps and how-to books, geography, geology, psychology and biographies. Garfy stopped to look for his biography. Yes, it was there. He very much approved of this bookshop!

There were windows across the whole of the front wall of this floor and each had two chairs and a table in front of them. It was perfect for people who wanted to linger over a novel or study history.

On the bottom floor was the poetry and fiction section. At the back, in the children's section, there was a family choosing from a pile leaning up against the back wall.

***

Garfy loved the peace and quiet of the place. He spent hours exploring all the nooks and crannies, sampling all the benches to snooze on and sitting on all the window seats to look out on the street. But Sam didn't like the fact that, at the moment, *quiet and peaceful* meant empty of people. He wanted the kind of peace that comes with children immersed in a new book and the quiet excitement in adults finding that their favourite author had written another book they hadn't yet read.

Not only did he want to share his love for books and stories with the rest of Ely, he wanted the business to be successful. Being successful meant money coming in. Money coming in meant people coming in and buying books.

***

When Garfy left that afternoon, full of sardines, he was a little worried. Would the shop be successful if Sam had so much to do? Was Mrs Muldoon a help or more of a hindrance? And what about all that scratching noise from you-know-who? Where was it coming from?

Garfy would have to find out the next time he visited. Maybe he could recruit a few people to help while he was at it.

***

The next day was Sunday and Garfy spent the day pacing up and down, trying to think of how he and his friends could help Sam get Robinson's Booksellers clean and tidy and selling lots of books.

Could Timmy Welch help? They stocked his book.

No, he was gardens.

But he knew he was on the right lines. An author maybe, to come and read from their book? If only he knew one.

***

That evening, as David and Garfy were snoozing together in the armchair, the phone rang with an urgency that made them both jump.

Garfy hopped onto the floor and tried to look as if he'd moved on purpose by starting to clean his back.

David got up to answer the phone. "Hello? Oh, hello, Sam." He listened for a long while. "I see… that is a shame… OK… No, I'm sure he will. I'll send him up tomorrow."

"Most intriguing," thought Garfy. Sam sounded like he was in a spot of bother. This was his chance to help!

David explained that the scratching noise Garfy had heard in the shop had been going on for a long time and Sam couldn't find out where it was coming from. As he was tidying up the corner of the fiction section, where books beginning with 'H' were kept, he discovered a hole in the wall. He shone a torch into the hole and there, staring straight back at him was a mouse – bold as you please!

Sam didn't know what to do. He didn't want mousetraps all over the place. What would people think? And who knows what little human fingers might get caught in them?

"Would you help out?" David asked. "They're keeping the customers away. I'm sure the mice would move straight out if they saw you walking about the shop."

Garfy wasn't so sure. He had spent his life trying to chase off mice and, while they scurried away if they saw him, they soon came back. It was as if they knew he was a friendly fellow and weren't particularly bothered by him.

But this was Sam so Garfy promised: he would do his best.

***

Now that Garfy knew where *Robinson's – Booksellers* was, he hopped on and off the bus quickly and was soon marching down the high street. He stepped into the bookshop only to find Mrs Muldoon, clutching her broom, standing tight up against a corner shelf staring wide-eyed at something on the floor. There, right in the middle of the shop, between fiction beginning with M and fiction beginning with E, was a mouse, with a smooth brown coat, large velvety ears and long tail, cleaning its whiskers.

"Rather brazen, aren't you?" said Garfy observed to it.

The mouse looked straight at him, shrugged and scurried off to the far side of the fiction section and squeezed between *The Tailor of Gloucester* and *The Rescuers.*

The ginger tom shook his head. "This isn't going to work," he thought.

***

Determined to do what he could to discourage the mice, Garfy set up sentry duty at the gap between the books where the mouse had disappeared. He waited and waited for what seemed like hours, but there wasn't a peep from any little creature – not even a bookworm.

Sam had managed to get the heating in the shop working again and it was getting cosy. That made Garfy sleepy. His eyes closed and his head began to nod. Then, just as he was about to drift off, out dashed a mouse.

The cheeky fellow been waiting the whole time, just the other side of the pile of books. He thought this was his chance and he made for the bookshelf on the other side of the shop. Garfy's acute ears heard the tiny patter of feet and his eyes sprang open.

With a jump, he shot off after the mouse, in hot pursuit.

***

Garfy raced up the stairs to the first floor, nearly catching the mouse's tail on the top step. The mouse leapt ahead, bounced off a map for the Norfolk Coastal Path and skittered over a small stack of books on decluttering. They fell from the top floor to the bottom, all the way down the stairs, taking with them two piles of atlases and four boxes of leaflets on health and safety.

Cat and mouse both headed into the corner, where Garfy thought he had the little intruder at last, pinned between books on mountaineering and leaflets on animal husbandry.

"You're keeping the customers away," he yowled. "Sam will have to close the shop for good if you don't move out!"

The mouse didn't seem to care. He scaled the books in a trice and bounded up the stairs to the second floor trying to find another hiding spot.

Garfy dashed after him. "You can't stay here. This is Sam's dream and you're ruining it!"

Garfy found the mouse perched on a huge blue book on sculptures. "This isn't your shop!" the mouse squeaked indignantly. "You've got Paterson's all to yourself. Why do you want to come here and claim this as your shop too?"

"It's not your shop either," Garfy pointed out, as he inched closer, his body hidden behind a stack of books on mazes. "It's Sam's shop. He's been waiting and saving for years to buy a bookshop and now, after tackling all the mess and the dust, he has to deal with a whole mischief of mice."

The mouse did begin to look a bit sorry but he was determined to stay. "It's alright for you," he said, "you have a home you can go back to every night. My whole family has nowhere else to go." And with that, he disappeared beyond the bookshelf on designer gardens, into the nearest hole in the wall.

Garfy stood still in his tracks. He didn't even consider where the mice would go if he chased them out. They would be homeless.

He went down the stairs to find Sam.

***

Downstairs, the chase among the books had caused quite a stir inside and outside the shop. Sam had come running to the bottom of the stairs, just as two people stepped over the threshold, attracted by the commotion.

They stared at the fallen books, then at Garfy, who had a sheepish look on his face.

Sam feared the worst. This would be the end of it all. He braced himself and went to apologise.

Before he could get a word out though, one of the people exclaimed, "Garfy! What have you been up to? Your old tricks again?" The couple laughed.

The other said thoughtfully, "What a lovely old shop. I haven't been in here since I was a lad."

They stepped further in. "Let's have a look around. Will you escort us, Garfy?"

Of course he would! What would they like? A map book of the British Isles – always a good seller. What about a romping romance – nice for some holiday reading? *The Bremmand Chronicles* – perfect for a wet weekend?

More people started to come in, curious to know what was going on to cause all this din.

When they stepped into the bookshop they forgot about the noise and wandered around picking up books and reading the backs of them, choosing what to buy for their trip, the grandchildren's birthday, a thank-you gift…

"What a lovely place," they all said and Sam, so knowledgeable about all the books, would help them find what they were looking for.

'Ah. Well if you like Jane Austen, have you tried…?" "No. The *Observer* books aren't in print any more but if you want a good book on butterflies…" "The next book in the *Fizz-wig* series is due out in September. I can pre-order it for you if you like."

All the seats and chairs and windowsills came in handy too. Garfy was so tired from showing people round, he would sometimes hop up onto one of the cushioned seats and have a quick catnap.

***

After that, people came from all over Ely and beyond, to visit Robinson's and see if they could seek out Garfy and find a treasure of a book too.

They'd find him on the top floor on the big blue cushion.

"Ooh!" they'd say, as they sat down next to him and the heaving shelves, "I always wanted to read about Frida Kahlo."

They'd seek him out on a windowsill on the bottom floor. "I didn't know they had a new book out," they'd say of their favourite author.

Wherever Garfy was, a book was sold. Sometimes two or more.

Sam's adventure into selling books was staring to pay off. The mice and Garfy had come in useful after all!

***

As for the mice: Garfy was no fighter, so he did the only thing he could do and that was negotiate.

They could stay on if they promised not to chew anything that was a book (or anything that was made out of paper for that matter). In exchange, Garfy would bring kibble, sardines and tea every Sunday and they would all sit and have their lunch together.

All sixty-seven (and counting) of them!

***

With the help of the Ely residents, who rediscovered their love of books and bookshops, the shed at the back of Robinson's was converted to a cat/dog zone, in line with the new mayor's initiative. There was also a special chair, just for Garfy.

Garfy, however, thought the chair was a bit too posh for him. He preferred to sit on all the other chairs and benches with the humans reading, absorbed in their wonderful world of books.

***

And Sam? Well, he still didn't get to spend all day reading because he was so busy helping other people enjoy the shop but he got to spend all day with books and that was just as good.

6

Hollywood Garfy

Garfy's fame continued to grow with each passing month. Tourism in Ely was booming and thousands of people around the world were following his adventures. Word spread and his exploits attracted the attention of CJ Millar from the west coast of America.

Now, CJ Millar heard it from his cousin, Wendell, who heard it from his business partner Maris, who heard it from her husband Royce, who heard it from his friend Audrey that there was a famous cat in England whose story would make a great movie.

CJ, the biggest movie mogul in Hollywood, read Garfy's biography and had one of his assistants gather all the stories they could about this charismatic cat and the way he made things happen to help his friends.

CJ thought – and all his assistants agreed – that someone should go and investigate. Usually one of the assistants would take on this duty – and they were all keen to volunteer for an all-expenses paid trip to England – but CJ was a cat-lover and he wanted to meet this intriguing feline. He was looking for a subject for his next blockbuster movie and he had a feeling this could be it.

He could already picture the posters on the sides of buses: *Garfy – The Movie!*

***

Garfy himself was blissfully unaware of the stir he was causing across the Atlantic. He was spending a very nice afternoon visiting Paterson's superstore, playing hide and seek on the shelves in the biscuit aisle with the children of some of the shoppers. The superstore was fairly quiet still. The school day had only just finished so only the parents of the nearest schools had made it to Paterson's for their weekly shop. It wouldn't be for another half an hour or so that it would get really busy. Garfy had plenty of time before he needed to walk down to the entrance to greet everyone.

***

It was a rarity to find David coming down to the store, so when Garfy saw him searching, wide-eyed, around the aisles, he feared the worst. Was it Sam? Had the mice started playing up again? Was it the twins? Had something happened to Morgan and Isabella? Were Kenji and Hana OK?

He sat up from behind the ginger nuts so he could be seen. David rushed up to him. "Oh, thank goodness

I've found you, Garfy. I've had a phone call; something's happened."

Garfy held his breath.

"They want to make a movie about you!" David said.

"A movie?" thought Garfy. "Who wants to make a movie about me?"

"CJ Millar is coming next week to visit you, to see if you'll star in it."

***

Garfy couldn't believe it. A movie mogul from America wanted to make a film about a cat from Ely? He stood there, high above the digestives and garibaldis, dumbstruck.

David snapped him out of his reverie. "Garfy! We need to prepare. Come on!"

***

Back home, David sped around the house picking things up, frowning at them and putting them down again. He was in a bit of a tizzy. Garfy watched him go this way and that. He still couldn't believe it.

David sat down next to him. "We need a plan," he said.

They made a list of all the places they had to tidy up and all the spaces they had to clean. Then they listed the food they thought a movie mogul would like to eat when he came. Caviar? Too expensive. Sushi? Too fiddly.

They settled for sandwiches and cake. "Everyone likes sandwiches, especially sardine ones," Garfy thought.

All week they spent cleaning and tidying. Garfy found his long-lost favourite toy under the sofa and David counted £4.72 from under the cushions. The place had never been so sparkling clean.

***

CJ Millar arrived at their door in a black limousine which was so long, it nearly stretched round the corner into the next street. Out stepped a man as broad as he was tall, with slicked-back hair and a long black jacket with the collar turned up. His sunglasses were enormous and hid not just his eyes but the whole upper half of his face.

He knocked on the door lightly while looking out onto the front garden, then turned around with his arms open wide as David opened it.

"You must be David! Great; wonderful!" Then, "Where's my star?" as he swept into the front room where Garfy stood to attention.

He had spent so long cleaning his bib and socks, he was quite tired from the exertion.

"Ah! Garfy, my boy! Great; wonderful!"

***

CJ spent most of the day studying Garfy and describing to David how the story would be told and discussing locations. He was going to make the elegant ginger cat into a star!

Garfy was both excited and terrified at the same time.

David was flabbergasted – so much so, he'd hardly said a word all day. He couldn't believe his cat, whom he'd had since he was a kitten, was going to feature in a movie!

***

The next day, CJ wanted to look at the list his location scout had sent him. They started in Daisy Down Park, walking from top to bottom. "This would be great for the scene where the helicopter chases you across the field. Great; wonderful!" said the movie mogul, sweeping his arms along the large open grass area.

Garfy was confused. He'd never been chased by a helicopter – although it did sound exciting.

Next, they moved onto Narrow Lane at the bottom of the park.

"Yes!" said CJ. "Great; wonderful! This is where you will scurry across the tops of the houses, along the rooftops, to find your sweetheart and help her escape from the clutches of the evil black cat, Tyson." Garfy had had a scuffle with Tyson in the past, when the black cat wanted to take over at Paterson's, but a sweetheart? Garfy blushed. It was all getting a bit too much.

***

They rode around for the rest of the day in CJ's limousine, looking out of the windows at various places around Ely (all of which CJ thought were *Great; wonderful!*), making notes and discussing contracts.

Garfy was really enjoying himself. He loved car rides and this one was beyond anything he'd ever been in before.

Finally, the day ended with a hand/paw shake, a final "Great; wonderful!" and the promise of paperwork within the week to sign, ready for a spring shoot. CJ would be back then but, in the meantime, he would be in touch about co-stars.

Garfy enjoyed being the centre of attention and listening to all these far-fetched adventures he was going to have. It was going to be such fun!

When, finally, they parked outside Garfy's house,

people walked past staring into the blacked-out windows of the limo, trying to see who was inside.

"Someone very famous, no doubt," they said.

Curtains twitched in the houses and walkers on the pavements slowed their pace to see if some celebrity would step out of the limo. The driver opened the back door, Garfy hopped out with a farewell "miaow!" and, with his nose and tail high in the air, he walked up to his front door.

People along the pavement looked at one another and whispered, "What's Garfy up to *this* time?"

***

The following week, CJ sent Garfy's main co-star to meet him. Cheryl Meep arrived, unannounced, in another stretch-limo, all in white. She swept around the car and up to the door, her long white coat flapping wide as she walked.

This time, when David answered the door, he nearly fainted! "H-h-hello, d-d-do come in." He did his best at keeping cool – though not very successfully.

Cheryl Meep was David's favourite actor. He had seen all her movies from when she first made it in Hollywood. He became a little starstruck.

"You were amazing in *Jacobs versus Jacobs*, and *Inside Asia* was *the* best film you've ever done," he gushed.

Cheryl waved the adoration away. "Thank you, darling, thank you! Just a jobbing actor, really."

Her attention turned to Garfy. "What a beautiful cat you have," she said, stroking him. "Elegant and refined. We are going to get on just marvellously." Her smile took in cat and owner.

They both swooned. What a day it was to have a famous actor in their house and eating the finger sandwiches that David made himself.

Cheryl Meep had shaken his hand in greeting and he was never going to wash it again![3]

***

She left a little while after the sandwiches, to stay at Ely House Hotel.

She held David's hand again in farewell. "So wonderful to meet you, David," she said, looking deep into his eyes.

David's knees went wobbly. "A-and you too, Miss Meep," he managed.

Then she turned to Garfy. "Garfield Abercrombie Reginald Fergusson, this will be my best movie yet, in part because you will be in it. I can't wait to work with you. It's going to be a *huge* hit!"

With that, she glided to the white limo and it drove away.

***

---

3   I don't know about you, but I really hope David DID wash his hand again. I mean... Urgh!

Was this really it? Was Garfy going to be *really* famous? Like Cheryl Meep? What would the people of Ely think? What would all his friends think? Could he go to Paterson's, the High Street and Robinson's without being mobbed by an adoring crowd, all clamouring for his autograph? Being in a movie was one thing, being famous was another thing entirely.

No, he was determined it wouldn't change him. He'd still be the ginger cat, elegant and refined, friend to all, chaser of mice.

***

Spring came around quicker than anyone thought was possible. Arrangements had been made for the film crew to set up outside the cathedral at the top of the hill and in the park next to Narrow Lane at the bottom. Roads were closed to accommodate filming and everywhere there were barriers and people in black outfits with walkie-talkies and the word *Crew* printed across the backs of their shirts.

Garfy had his own trailer to sit in while he waited for his scenes, where two humans would brush his fur and dust the tip of his nose with powder. But all that luxury was nothing compared to the huge trailer for Cheryl Meep and the people who milled about her all the time.

As Garfy explored his trailer on the first day – there was a well-stocked fridge which he promised he would sample later – a tiny little knock came at the door.

It opened outwards to reveal… no one!

Garfy looked around. Was it David trying to get in? Were the crew ready for his first scene?

He was just about to shut the door again, when he heard a voice.

"Down here!"

On the bottom step leading up to the trailer was a cat, smaller than Garfy, but with the same ginger stripes down her back and the same white bib and socks.

"I'm Gillian St. Jude Atkinson Stanley, your co-star," she said. "Everyone calls me Gill."

Wow! Garfy was dumbstruck.

"I'm…" he began with a stammer but she held up a paw.

In a voice full of awe, she said, "I know who you are. You're the famous Garfy. So nice to meet you finally. I read your biography as soon as it came out. You've had such adventures. I'm so excited to work with you."

It was her turn to swoon in front of him. She was clearly a huge fan and starstruck in his presence.

In turn, Garfy was a little overwhelmed. Not because cats and humans were starting to treat him differently because of his fame, although that did have some bearing. It was because his heart leapt as soon as he saw Gill. She was lovely.

Garfy soon discovered throughout the day that she was smart and funny too. He'd never met such a cat. I think it's safe to say, he had something of a crush!

It turned out that Cheryl Meep was playing Gill's human in the movie and the three of them would be working together for the whole week. Garfy couldn't believe his luck!

What a wonderful week it was.

Garfy loved working with Gill but, more than that, they would spend all their breaks together in his trailer, laughing and telling stories.

Gill was from the nearby town of Soham and got the job in the movie by beating fifty other cats in the auditions.

Garfy could listen to her all day. He sat staring at her, with his head in his paw. She would do the same when he told her of his adventures and escapades in Ely. She especially loved the story about his fight with Tyson.

Of course, Garfy had forgotten: Tyson would be in the movie too. He wasn't looking forward to that!

***

As they prepared for the scene when Garfy found Gill and together they got away from Tyson, Garfy became more and more anxious about the arrival of the big black bully of a cat. Tyson hadn't arrived yet, however, and waiting for him wasn't helping Garfy's nerves.

What would he say to him after all this time? Would he be able to stand up to Tyson if the bullying started again?

He was soon to find out. A human came up to the group with a cat carrier. Inside, all Garfy could see was a huge black shadow pacing up and down.

This was it! Garfy tried to stop his knees from knocking in terror.

The door to the carrier was unlocked and out jumped…

"Hi! I'm Gus. I'll be playing Tyson."

What a relief! It wasn't Tyson after all. This experienced stunt-cat, Gus, would be playing him instead.

The three cats got on famously for the rest of the movie. The action scenes, although far-fetched and not resembling anything that happened in real life, were a lot of fun. Even the helicopter chase across Daisy Down Park was exhilarating, despite all the noise and downdraft!

The whole experience was almost as good as Garfy's adventures and it was made all the more interesting because of Gill.

***

All too soon, shooting was over and, in the space of a day, the crew packed up all their trailers and film equipment and were gone.

Garfy and Gill stood alone on the empty ground next to the cathedral, gazing at the crushed grass and tyre tracks which were all that was left of the film set.

"It was so nice working with you," Gill said as her human waited to one side with her cat basket.

"Let's do it again sometime!" said Garfy. "You're not too far away. I could get David to bring me to see you in Soham."

With that, they walked off toward their respective humans, each looking over their shoulder as they went their separate ways.

***

Garfy had really enjoyed being an actor, although he had discovered that the movie-making business wasn't nearly as glamorous as it looked from the outside. It had been hard work and, while it had been interesting, he didn't think the actor's life was him. All the same, he did miss the hustle and bustle of learning lines and acting and re-takes, and now he felt rather flat.

Most of all, though, he missed Gill. They'd had such a wonderful time together, he didn't want it to end.

End it did, however, as does every excitement, and life in Ely was getting back to normal.

The film was due to come out ready for Christmas, so CJ and his team had a lot of work to do back in Hollywood to make that happen. Back on the West Coast, editing and effects and music were all being added to create *the next great CJ Millar blockbuster.*

***

Garfy didn't hear from anyone in an age, so it was a surprise when a sparkling white envelope arrived in the post in late November. It was edged in gold and was addressed to him.

It read, "Millar Productions cordially invites Garfield Abercrombie Reginald Fergusson and guest to the premiere of *Garfy, the Ely Years* at the Dolby Theatre, Hollywood, on December 18th."

Garfy was going to Hollywood!

A chauffeur would collect David and Garfy and take them to the airport, where they would fly first class all the way to America.

They would have a tour of the sights, then, in the evening, would be escorted to the premiere by CJ and Cheryl.

It was all too exciting!

But Garfy couldn't help thinking about one thing – or rather, one cat. He wished Gill could be there too.

***

The journey to America was luxurious. Garfy and David were treated like royalty.

They were escorted through airports and on and off planes.

Garfy had the highest-quality fish and kibble during the flight. He'd never felt so spoiled. He'd even been given a brand-new suitcase with G.A.R.F. in gold lettering on the side.

Travelling was tiring though, and Garfy was obliged to stay in his cat basket for rather a lot of the time so that made it a bit boring.

***

Soon enough, the aeroplane was touching down on the runway and one of CJ's assistants was there to greet them.

Garfy and David were staying in the best hotel on Sunset Boulevard and the assistant, Esther, was to take them straight there to get freshened up. After that, the tour started.

When Garfy entered the hotel, a hush came over the foyer and the reception staff came out from behind the front desk to make a fuss of him.

"Mr Fergusson, sir. It is our pleasure to have you stay at our hotel. This way. You have a priority booking. Everything is arranged."

They took his suitcase and carried it to the lift that took him to his room.

No one took the slightest notice of David. He had to carry his own suitcase and he almost didn't make it into the lift with Garfy.

In Hollywood, movie stars are everything; no one else even exists!

***

Garfy had never seen a room like that hotel room. It was, in fact, a suite of rooms.

There was a baby grand piano in the corner of the lounge and a fully stocked fridge nearby. There was a full choice of meats and cat biscuits and treats so delicate they melted on the tongue. His food bowl was made out of gold and his water bowl had diamonds encrusted round the edge.

Garfy stood astounded by the extravagance. He hopped lightly onto the windowsill and gazed out.

Across the city streets, in the distance, he could see the Hollywood sign, deep in the hills. It looked a bit wonky to the elegant cat who liked to have the stripes down his back in smart straight lines.

It made him smile to think about them. He was quite keen to see what his ginger stripes looked like on the big screen.

After a lovely long nap and a light snack, Garfy was ready to explore. He was eager to find out how different Hollywood was to Ely.

***

Boy, was it different!

Everything was so much bigger – cars, shops, food! All the sights seemed bigger too.

Ely had a cathedral it was true, but Hollywood had a hundred more attractions.

People didn't seem as friendly as Garfy was used to either, but they were still in awe of him. Everywhere he went, they cuddled him and stroked him and asked for his autograph.

He soon discovered why he was recognised everywhere. The first stop on his exclusive tour of Hollywood was Sunset Strip.

There, his face was on every billboard and on every bus that went by. Everywhere was advertising for his film. On walls and on the sides of buildings was his huge great profile with whiskers that must have been eight feet long!

Garfy was not only famous in Ely and the UK, he was famous all around the world. Fame was quite different in America, as Garfy was about to find out.

***

Next stop on the tour was the Capitol Records building. Garfy was as unimpressed with this as he was the wonky Hollywood sign. The building looked like an enormous scratching post only it was made of concrete so he couldn't use it.

Next came Hollywood Boulevard. Now, *this* was more impressive. There on the pavement (though the guide kept calling it a 'sidewalk'), there were thousands of stars with famous people's names in them. How wonderful it would be to have Garfield Abercrombie Reginald Fergusson written in a star one day.

If the film was a hit, maybe that would happen.

***

After that, he walked around outside Grauman's Chinese Theatre, where hundreds of actors and famous people had put their hand and footprints into wet concrete at the theatre's entrance. Maybe, after Garfy had starred in several films, he'd have his paw prints embedded there too.

A car had its tyre prints there and a horse his hoofprints so it didn't seem so far-fetched that his paws would be there for all to see. Millions of people would go there every year to take photographs of his prints, with 'Garfy' written in the concrete. Millions! Would he enjoy being that famous?

***

Although he loved the tour, he didn't see why people made such a huge fuss about the place – or such a fuss about him, either.

His fame had certainly reached Hollywood, even before the film aired, but he was just a cat – a handsome one who was pretty good acting, he thought – but a cat nonetheless. Yes, people had heard about his adventures but that was all.

It seemed a little unreal to him. He certainly didn't understand the fuss when anyone recognised him.

In the UK he would get a smile, a greeting and maybe someone would politely ask if they could have his autograph.

Here, though, fans would sweep in, scoop him up without asking, scream, call all their friends over, take a hundred photos and then ask him if he knew some other celebrity (usually someone he'd never even heard of) he could introduce to them.

It was exhausting, somewhat unsettling and most undignified. He was missing David's lap in their cosy Ely home, even if he did have to fight a newspaper for it sometimes.

***

That evening, after a long nap and supper, CJ's assistant, Esther, knocked on the door. She was carrying a parcel in one hand and a phone in the other.

On the other end of the phone was CJ. "It's all over the news!" he said. "You are the next big hit, Garfy. This hasn't happened since Herby the car, in the 1970s. It's great; wonderful!"

CJ went on to explain that on nearly every TV channel was the news that the elegant ginger cat was in town to attend the premiere of his movie. "I'll be sending a car soon, to pick you up. Charles will be riding with you. He's your new bodyguard. You'll need one now. He'll be the start of your team and we'll interview for a PA, a manager and agent next week. Great; wonderful!"

Garfy's excitement began to fade. Why would he need all these people around him? A bodyguard to keep people from screaming too close to him and picking him up during his trip was one thing but a PA and a manager?

Where were they going to stay? His house in Ely wasn't that big – not while he allowed David to live there too.

Esther rubbed his head. "Don't worry, Garfy, you'll settle in Hollywood really quickly. Most people do."

With that she unwrapped the parcel to reveal Garfy's outfit for the night.

***

Now, we all know that Garfy is refined and elegant but the contents of the parcel were a bit much.

It was a tuxedo! A little dinner jacket, shirt, bowtie and trousers for his big night.

Garfy couldn't cope. No one would see the smart stripes which he'd spent so long grooming.

***

A long red carpet had been laid outside the Dolby Theatre that night and an enormous crowd had gathered behind ropes.

Garfy was used to crowds in Ely – all his escapades recently seemed to have attracted them – but he had never seen so many people waiting for him. They were pushing and jostling for the best view so they could take photos when the stars got out of their limos. It was pandemonium.

Garfy stared out of his limo window, Charles by his side. "It gets easier," the big bodyguard consoled, "once you've been here a couple of years."

Everything Garfy was being told was making him sadder and sadder. A couple of years? He missed home, he missed Paterson's and his friends. He even missed the hundreds of mice he had been feeding at Robinson's.

He didn't want to stay here and have to be guarded and organised and managed.

He wanted to roam the city he was born in, visit his friends when he wanted and eat sardines and kibble out of his own bowl. It would soon be Christmas and tinsel, his favourite cat toy, would be stocked to the ceilings in Paterson's. Father Christmas would be visiting too and he didn't want to miss that.

***

"Sunglasses on," said Charles, as they stepped out of the limo. "All those camera flashes will hurt your eyes."

The noise was incredible.

Everyone was shouting his name. "Garfy! Over here! What do you think of America so far?" asked a reporter.

"Great," thought Garfy, "but could everyone stop screaming?" He couldn't hear himself think!

Cheryl had arrived, smiling and waving at the crowd. She stopped a little time with the reporters to answer one or two questions, then disappeared into the theatre. She made it look easy.

Garfy didn't think he would ever get used to it. People were still shouting his name and he couldn't think of answers to their questions quick enough before they started asking the next one. It was becoming very confusing.

Garfy felt a little faint. All the lights, the noise, his silly tuxedo – it was all too much.

***

Just then, he saw Gill in the crowd.

Garfy's heart skipped a beat.

She looked beautiful in a little chiffon dress and diamond necklace. Gill's human was just behind her but with all the crowds of people, she was being swept past him too quickly, and he only managed to call out to her once.

"Hi, Garfy!" she called back. "You do look smart! Off home tomorrow, see you soon…"

CJ came up to him to escort him to the entrance of the theatre. "Garfy, you're set for life here. Great; wonderful! I'm thinking franchise, merchandise... three or four films... apartment in Los Angeles, maybe one in New York..."

That was the last straw. Tuxedos and sunglasses, apartments, film after film, work, work, work... *and* he couldn't even get to speak to Gill. No thank you!

Not for Garfy.

***

The film couldn't end soon enough. There was supposed to be a party afterwards but Garfy excused himself to 'freshen up'.

He took off his tuxedo and sunglasses and left them on the ground in the corridor as he slipped away. Once he was in the foyer, he made a dash for it out across the red carpet which was looking a little strange on the pavement now the crowd had gone home. He ran to his limo and ducked down, so no one would see him leave.

***

Back at the hotel, he sat forlornly on one of the seats, wondering how on *earth* he was going to get out of this one.

Then he heard the key in the door and, determined not to be made to go back, he hid under the bed.

In came David with Garfy's tuxedo in his hands.

"Garfy," came the familiar voice. "Are you here?"

Garfy poked his nose out, not sure if he was going to be forced back into that horrible outfit.

David dropped to his knees and gathered Garfy up in his arms. "Oh, *Garfy!*" he said. "I'm so glad to see you are safe. What a crazy place. Let's get out of here."

***

Together they packed Garfy's gold-lettered suitcase, hurried back out into the limo and were soon racing towards the airport to catch the next flight home.

As soon as he was in his seat and the cabin crew were doing their pre-flight checks, Garfy began to breathe easily again.

He shook his head. An actor's life wasn't for him. He wanted peace and quiet, naps and friends – old friends like the people who worked at Paterson's, Sam, Morgan and Isabella, Salty, Kenji and Hana; new friends like Ali and Caroline, and, of course, Gill.

***

After what seemed like days, Garfy was home – standing in his front garden, staring at the front door. David opened it and stepped aside to allow his elegant ginger tom in first.

Garfy sniffed at it for a moment but then turned and, at a swift trot, headed down the hill to the homeware aisle of Paterson's and his favourite bale of towels. *Now* he was home!

***

Movie fame didn't touch Garfy at all. If you go to Paterson's even today, he'll be around somewhere. If he isn't asleep on a shelf or waiting at the entrance to say hello, you might find him at Robinson's Booksellers instead.

He'll be about somewhere because Garfy is always there for his friends.

If you want an autograph he will purr and oblige – giving you a head nuzzle too, if you are lucky. He is always happy to meet the fans.

This is as far as it goes, however, for this is Garfield Abercrombie Reginald Fergusson, an elegant ginger tom with a white bib and socks and some elegant stripes down his back. He's no movie star for he is *Ely's* most famous cat and that is what he is loved for.

And as for Gill? Well, that's another story!

About Garfy

Garfield (aka Garfy) was a *real* ginger tom, widely known as 'Ely's most famous cat'. In 2012, a new Sainsbury's in Ely was built on the site of an old factory. This was land which had been Garfield's roaming ground previously, so he simply continued to visit. As a result, he became well known by customers of the supermarket and something of a local celebrity.

Some of his fans and his owner, David, set up a Facebook page (https://www.facebook.com/The1mrsainsburys) and his fame spread worldwide, with many appearances in local and national media. He became the 'pin-up' cat for the local Cat's Protection who claim he has saved them over £1,000 in cat food because customers at Ely's Sainsbury's donated food due to the 'Garfield factor'.

On 2nd July 2019 Garfield was hit by a car in the Sainsbury's car park and died from his injuries. His loss was felt by everyone who visited the supermarket and everyone whose life had been touched by this extraordinary cat grieved for him.

But his memory lives on. Garfy had so many adventures that we wanted to keep sharing his story. Every one of the stories you read here is based (sometimes very loosely!) on a real adventure Garfield has had.

Other Garfy Books

What's THAT doing there?

Available in print and as an audiobook.

Garfy, full name Garfield Abercrombie Reginald Fergusson, is an elegant ginger tom with white bib and socks who lives in Ely. He loves to roam in the large meadow opposite his home. Then, one day, someone puts up fences and builds a Paterson's Superstore on Garfy's meadow.

What is a cat to do? Garfy adopts the supermarket as his home from home and is their first customer. He rapidly becomes a celebrity cat, loved by the customers and full of mischief.

This collection of short stories, illustrated by Ginny Phillips, features the fictionalised adventures of the real Garfield, Ely's most famous cat!

A Tribute to Garfield

Cate Caruth

Given at the Pet Service in
Ely Cathedral – 22nd September 2019

What is it about our pets?

How is it that they become so much a part of our lives?

What makes us so besotted with these creatures which are, genetically speaking, nothing like us?

And yet we are.

We are crazy about our pets.

We love them. We take thousands of photographs of them. They are a constant feature on our Facebook feeds, on Instagram and Twitter, and in our conversations.

They rule our lives and our homes.

Anyone who isn't a 'pet person' must look at us and think we are completely bonkers.

But it doesn't bother us for a moment. We are proud to be a *dog nut* or a *crazy cat lady*. It doesn't worry us that everybody else is terrified of our tarantula. We don't care if the only person who thinks our gecko is beautiful is us.

Our pets are not just an addition to our family, they are part of our family.

***

And then, every now and again, a pet comes along who is a member of all of our families.

Every now and again there is a pet like Garfield.

Garfield Abercrombie Reginald Fergusson was an elegant ginger cat with a white bib and socks and some very smart stripes down his back. He was cheeky and clever and mischievous and, all in all, a bit of a rogue.

He was known – and rightly so – as Ely's most famous cat.

He first came to attention when Sainsbury's opened their new supermarket on Lisle Lane. Before that it had been a brownfield site where Garfield liked to wander. When they built the supermarket on it, Garfield simply carried on wandering there.

The curiosity that all cats are famous for, led him into car boots, shopping bags, boxes and inside the store. People started buying treats for him when they did their weekly shopping.

Garfield started to get so stout that, under vet's instructions, David (his owner) was obliged to ask Sainsbury's to put up a notice saying, "Please do not feed this cat."

***

Now Garfield got *really* famous. The local press saw the sign, were amused and printed a story about him. And then another, and then another, and then another…

Garfield enjoyed celebrity – in fact he rather courted it, and he certainly made the most of everyone who came to the Sainsbury's in Ely to see him.

He became an advocate for the local Cats Protection. Their donation box at Sainsbury's saved them around £1,000 a year in cat food. He made appearances at their cat show every year and, by bringing people to the show, helped to find homes for other cats.

He was truly loved by everyone who knew him.

***

This was where I came in. I'm not from Ely. I didn't know about Garfield. But I have friends who live there and who knew I was a writer – as well as a crazy cat lady. So they put me in touch with David who wanted to create a book about his cheeky cat and the adventures he got up to.

The more I got to know Garfield and got to know about the stories that so enchanted people, the more I too fell in love with him. He was charming to look at and knew it. In fact, he was an outrageous flirt.

But he was a writer's gift – and *What's That Doing There?* was one of the easiest books I've ever written.

***

Through the pages of the book, through his Facebook page, through public appearances, and through his antics in and around the Sainsbury's supermarket, Garfield touched thousands of lives around the world. He was a pet for those who could have no pet of their own and, for Tina and David, he was family.

***

To lose a pet is always sad. To lose one suddenly and unexpectedly can be particularly hard. When Garfield was hit by a car and died from his injuries on the 2nd of July 2019, the whole of Ely mourned for him. The flowers and gifts, the generous donations and the loving comments that so many people have made since he died have been so touching and just go to show how great his impact was.

He was gone too soon. There were still so many stories we had to tell about him. And there were so many lives that he was yet to touch.

For those who knew him best, he has left a hole that is impossible to fill.

He was, quite simply, our lovely handsome boy and we are so very grateful that we had the opportunity to have him in our lives.

***

But this isn't just a eulogy for Garfield. This is a moment for us all to spare a thought for anyone who is grieving the loss of a pet.